FROM DARKNESS

Fated Soules Series Book One

FROM DARKNESS

Jan Lindie

Fated Soules Series

Book One

REDHAWK
PUBLICATIONS

Redhawk Publications
2550 US Hwy 70 SE
Hickory, NC 28602
Attn: Robert Canipe
rcanipe@cvcc.edu

ISBN: 978-1-952485-00-8
All art, including the cover art, was done by Jan Lindie.
For permission to use art please email her at:
JustJansArt@gmail.com

For Betty Jane (Soule) Lindie

Whose unconditional love and support gave me the will to follow my Dreams. I did it Mom! I wish you were here to share this with me in person, but I know you are with me in my heart and soule, Always... I Love and Miss you, Mom! Also I want to dedicate this to my amazingly talented sister Karen Elizabeth (Lindie) Kinder, whose art was always so inspiring and beautiful. I wish we could have drawn together. I love you, Sis.

You both lived with love and dedication. Which is still felt by the ones you have left behind.

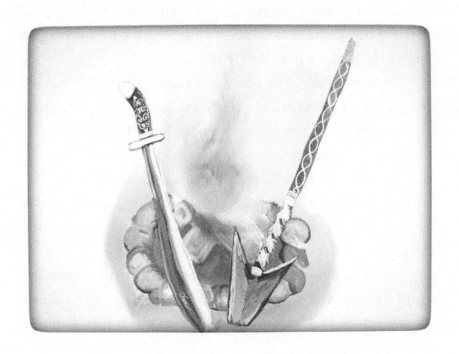

Prologue

The year was 219 BCE... it was the year that changed everything... I remember that night like it was only yesterday and not two thousand two hundred and thirty-six years ago.

Smoke billowed from the water-soaked campfire; the army would have to douse the flames quicker than that if they wanted to hide themselves in their ingenious smoke screen. Ingenious in my mind because it was my love's idea. The enemy was coming, of this there certainly was no doubt. It was only a matter of time. Wu Xia held his men at the ready as I hovered near.

Being a goddess, even a lesser one (for I was just a daughter of the God and Goddess of love), in a time of war should have been a boon to these warriors, but I wasn't here to decide the course of this battle. I was here as punishment for once again falling in love with a mortal.

In my defense it was the same mortal... It was always the same mortal. A different name, but he always had the same soule, same eyes, same face, and same amazing heart. His sincerity and noble honor shown like a beacon. Not only to me but to all who were around him in whatever lifetime he regenerated in. Reincarnation, while not always timely, was at least one way of ensuring that the soule of my dearest love would always come back to me.

But I had been foolish this time around. Instead of guarding my heart and emotions I put them on display, and for doing so I was forced by Longwei to this spot to watch this lifetime's untimely end.

I swore that I wouldn't leave Wu Xia. No matter the cost.

Hush my love they are near. I whispered into his ear. Being this close to Xia, closer now than I had ever dared before, while he was awake anyways, was the only solace I could offer him. *I won't leave your side. Not until your body is taken away by the worms and darkness has eaten away at the light that is my soule.*

Longwei's decree still rang in my ears. This would be the last reincarnation Xia would ever have. Longwei wouldn't put up with my flagrant disregard for his laws. I would atone for my sin for eternity.

Xia stood in the thick smoke his face covered in a strip of fine silk moistened in water from the nearby pond. Even in this dense darkness I could still see the bright aura that surrounded him, it was what made his soule so unmistakably that of Su Yang.

Su Yang, the name he was called when I first fell in love

with him. When he offered himself up for marriage to the evil Le Zhou's daughter instead of his elder brother. It was then that I felt the world tilt and the birds truly sing.

Yang, thinking his name alone brings me back to those days, to when he planted the most beautiful Cherry tree. The blossoms of which he once said were the most beautiful color of pale pink he had ever beheld. It was then that I changed my eyes into that very color. For I wanted him to think of me that way: Beautiful.

I care not what Longwei ordered, my thoughts pounded in my head echoing the thundering beats of my breaking heart. *I will never stop loving you...* the words had barely taken form in my mind before a single diamond tear began to roll down my cheek.

The tears of the gods aren't like those of a mortal. They are measured by the weight of their sorrow and take the form of precious metals and stones, and not the salty liquid tears that the mortals pour forth. Not once in my existence (and I have experienced many centuries of heartache) had I ever felt this much emotional pain.

A lone silver spear spiraled through the air slowly. Had it not been the work of a god's decree, the warrior who had thrown the spear would be celebrated as quite the marksman. But this was no skilled warrior but the ordained cruel torture that Longwei was doling out to me. I wept as Xia fought off attackers left and right. Unaware of the spear that was destined to take his life.

I don't know why, even now, I attempted to stop the spear with my body. I knew that the weapon would phase through me without even a scratch to myself. At that moment I only knew that I had to hold him, to try to shield him and at the very least, comfort him in his last moments on this earth. My teardrop fell from my face a fraction of a second before the spear flew through me on its wretched ordained path into the beautiful beating heart of Xia.

It was almost as if at that very moment time stood still. The battle around us ceased, the smoke seemed to disappear. The only sound to be heard for miles around was that of my heartrending cry:

I love you...

Xia's eyes grew wide; at the time I could only guess that they widen in recognition that the end was drawing near. His large brown eyes, which had been filled with determination a moment ago, softened into such tenderness that I had never seen before. His eyes slowly moved, searching the area around him for a few minutes before settling on the spot where I stood before him. His blood covered lips stretched into a faint smile, it lasted only for a heartbeat before his trembling lips parted. He spoke briefly before collapsing onto the ground and his once brilliant eyes dimmed forever.

That moment is etched into my very being, yet, his last words have haunted me every day for over two thousand years. Right up until the day that I never could have dreamed would possibly happen. The day that a blazing beacon woke me from a self-induced slumber-- The day that Yahui was born.

"Your eyes... they are so beautiful..."

Chapter 1

spent nearly three hundred years just existing. Going through the motions without really paying much attention to what I was doing. My followers started to forget about me right at the renewal of the world. It was then that I started to slumber. I found that I could still answer the true disciples, but it was growing less likely that the old ways were being honored. So, I locked myself away to wait until the end of time.

At first, all I could see was the darkness. Because that was the only thing that was left. A void that was torn into my very existence the moment Longwei, the High Lord of the Gods, stole away my love.

Two thousand two hundred and ten years is a long time to wait for a miracle. Yet a miracle is the only way that I can describe the course of events that took place that September day in the year 1991.

It all started with a flicker, a tiny spark of light that flashed before my slumbering eyes. A burning ember that was barely there hanging on for dear life, waiting ever so patiently for the spark to be fanned into a roaring flame.

Hmmm...Perhaps I'm not describing this at all correctly. Imagine, if you will, closing your eyes while you are in a completely darkened room.

Can you imagine that?

Yes?

Good...

Now imagine someone attempting to light a match while a high-speed fan is blowing overhead. It might spark but it fails to catch. You can see the slight flashes of light, but it fades nearly as fast as it starts. Now picture a flash of lightning that strikes just outside your window onto an old dead tree. The Flash alone is blinding, but the flame that remains continues to burn. Mesmerizing you, forcing you to take notice.

That is how I was awoken.

Brought back from the darkness, brought back to life.

I dared to hope. For hope was all that my weary soule could manage. After all that time slumbering, I was so weak. Yet, I felt the presence of a whisper. Somewhere in the world someone was praying to me, to me: Zhen'ai, the goddess of *Duijiē huì*. It was this whisper that made it possible to move, to follow the path that brought me back into the light.

It's now nearing the end of 2017 and it is from Darkness my life truly...begins.

§

For as long as I live, I will never forget the intoxicating aroma that first morning I woke up in my new form. My nostrils were enticed by the scents of Cherry blossoms and Lotus flowers. A gift from my dear caretaker, Ayi, I was sure.

I knew that Ayi had been worrying over me for weeks prior to the change and the thoughtful meaning behind each flower had my lips curling up into a peaceful smile. I had no doubt this was Ayi's way of enriching and blessing this new body while I transformed. I could feel my heart lighten from this thoughtful gift.

Soft silk sheets caressed my flesh as I remained cocooned in their luxury, I gently stretched my stiff body feeling each muscle tighten and release with the effort. I dared not open my eyes for I feared that I would find this all just a wondrous dream. That I was still unchanged, and I would never be able to truly live and love. It seemed like hours and not mere seconds that I remained laying there taking in my surroundings using only my new senses of touch and smell.

Yet, my careful movements, had not gone unnoticed.

"Thank the Gods, my Lady." Ayi's congenial voice startled me from my respite. I don't know how I missed her entry into the room. Perhaps I had lost all my godly prowess, an unforeseen side effect from the process. "It is time to wake up, my Lady. It is the morning of the twenty-sixth of December."

Blinking my eyes slowly open I allow them to adjust to the harsh morning light. Gazing at the beautiful drapery of the Cherry Blossoms and Lotuses; my breath hitched at the astonishing sight. It must have taken her days to weave them together like that. Let alone the amount of time it had taken in finding so many of the breathtaking blooms. Especially as they are not in season. *How long had I been asleep?* My bed's canopy held hundreds of beautiful flowers each vine draped over the carved wooden posts and beams.

"Oh my Lady... It is so good to see you finally awake." concern echoed in her every word. I let my eyes come to rest on her face. The twenty-sixth, which means I've been out for three weeks. No wonder she looked older in this light; her gentle face was lined with the concern that was echoed in her voice. Making her wrinkles stand out even more than normal. Her beautiful silver hair was pulled up into a disheveled bun, so unlike her usual neat knot I was accustomed to her wearing.

"Oh, my dear Ayi... I had wondered why I didn't hear your arrival. Now I can see the reason plainly. Have you stayed by my side this whole time?" my throat was so dry that my voice was raspy and harsh.

"Nearly my Lady. I have had to take care of other things. But I stayed close... you have never been left unattended." Ayi's eyes lowered to her hands.

"Thank you..." My voice cracked once again this time I began to cough from the dryness... I felt like the desert had taken over my mouth and throat. Clutching my neck with my long slender hand, I silently hoped that this wasn't what my voice would truly sound like...

Ayi rose from a chair that she had placed next to the head of the bed and walked over to the dresser where a pitcher of water sat with two glasses. With well-practiced grace she poured water into one of the glasses, setting the pitcher down she turned on her heel with the fluidity of a woman half her age, and brought its crystal clear liquid to me.

"Here my Lady, drink this before you say another word. You are parched, it has been weeks after all. The minerals in the water will also help to hydrate your body." Her stern eyes raked over me quickly before she opened her mouth to continue. "You can chastise me once you are fully hydrated and nourished." Her hand shook only slightly as she extended the glass towards me.

My fingers found the glass cool to the touch and I sat up before placing its rim to my lips. It was crisp and refreshing. I detected a small hint of a flavor that pulled at my memories, mint? There was mint in the water, I smiled broadly, she had remembered that I wanted to try it. After all the lifetimes of watching my love, my soulmate if you believe in that possibility, drink his water with mint added, I was now able to fully enjoy it myself. The aroma of the mint was heavenly.

"Drink that up." Ayi added looking quickly at her wristwatch. "I'm going to wake up the cook. She will be pleased to hear that you are finally up and wanting food."

"I never said that I was hungry. Don't..." But my villainous stomach rumbled in protest of my boldfaced lie.

Ayi's eyebrows arched as she smiled, shaking her head. "Not hungry, huh? I think that we both know better than that."

My cheeks flushed as I brought the glass back to my lips in a failed attempt to hide my embarrassment.

Traitorous stomach. I thought as Ayi's sheepish smile made me feel a strange growing sensation deep in my chest, the more I sat looking at Ayi and my glass the sensation grew, and grew, until finally a soft giggle escaped from my lips. The sound of which reminded me of the sound of the wind chimes up at the temple. I had to cover my mouth to stem the sound.

"Don't fret. I shall return soon with your breakfast and some clothes. After you eat you can bathe and get dressed. There is much to do to get ready for the night of the thirty-first, and precious little time to prepare." Without waiting for my response, she exited the room. I heard the bedroom door click shut before I placed my now empty glass on the nightstand.

She was right of course. I had planned on having nearly a month to prepare. Now we only had five days. Five days to acclimate myself to this new form.

My new form... Hmmm... I suppose seeing as I am all alone, I can take full stock of myself. Reluctantly I pushed the silk sheet off of my lap, where it had slid to when I sat up, before easing my bare legs over the side of the high bed. There was a full-length mirror just on the other side of the room. How hard could it be to walk over to view my own reflection?

The transformation process had certainly been *complicated* to say the least. What with so many things that could have gone wrong. The fact that I had been out for so many days... quite honestly was a little alarming to me. Undoubtedly it had been much longer than I had originally been told. *Had I done something wrong? Was the incantation spoken incorrectly?* My mind raced with all the possibilities, both good and bad... I couldn't help but wonder what I looked like. A slight giggle passed over my lips. *No doubt a mess. Much like my voice was when I first spoke.*

On wobbly legs I stood for the first time. For the first time... Such a strange concept seeing that my true age has never really been calculated. Plus, the fact that I had stood and walked for millennia. Even in a semi human form... But never truly like this. The cold wooden floorboards sent a burst of shivers over my skin. The sensation was enjoyable if not new. Never before had *standing* made me feel in such a way. Slipping my foot forward I took my first shaky step away from the bed. *One small step...* I smiled at that thought. Blue satin fabric, which was once supported by the mattress, cascaded down over my waist falling in fluid waves to stop just above my wobbly knees.

I never would have thought that the deep royal blue color would work with my skin tone, seeing as my original skin was more translucent then a true color. But, from the way that my nightgown looked against the bare flesh above my full breasts, I might seriously need to reconsider that notion. After a succession of unsure steps, I finally stood in full view of the mirror.

The young woman reflected there wasn't like anything I thought I would see. Truthfully, I'm not sure what I expected. After lying in bed for so many days without food, water, or any other necessities... I certainly didn't expect to see the youthful radiant vision of health that stared wide eyed back at me. Long flowing chestnut hair with honey colored highlights, my pale pink cherry blossom colored eyes had been replaced by a more natural but still alluring Amber.

I must have lost track of time on my trek from the bed to the mirror because before I could inspect further the bedroom door creaked open and Ayi's voice filled the room.

"Cook was up and already..." The sound of her voice came just before she could completely enter, carrying a tray filled to the edges with food. Food... The mouth-watering aroma was another sensation that I had never experienced before, at least not like this.

I turned quickly to face Ayi. Her voice froze in her throat, and she gazed at me as if she had never seen me before... At least that is what I thought until she found her voice again.

"My Lady!! Why are you out of bed? You should've waited until I was here to assist you."

The pure look of apprehension that appeared on Ayi's face caused me to regret my hasty decision.

"I am sorry, Ayi. I just wanted to..." looking over my shoulder at my reflection in the mirror. "I just wanted to see myself for the first time. Please forgive my impatience."

Ayi's reflections strode into view next to my own and she nodded before she wrapped her now empty arms around my waist. Whether she intuitively knew what was about to happen or my body just instinctively responded to her touch, quite honestly I am unsure which, but my knees buckled giving way and Ayi's arms had to support me, guiding me back over to the soft comfort of the bed.

"My Lady is stubborn; it might be wise to postpone the upcoming activities..."

"NO!"

The forcefulness of my response jumped even me. Let alone Ayi. I took a calming breath before responding in a much quieter tone. "It has to be the night of the thirty-first. I know you are worried my dear Ayi, but if this is to work, I must be seen by him on that night. Regardless of the little time that we have to prepare. If not..." my voice trailed off, but my mind continued my unspoken words. *If not, I will resort back into my ethereal form and fade away.* I wagered everything on this. I couldn't mess it all up with a case of weak knees.

I couldn't say that out loud. Ayi knew that this was unprecedented, but she was unaware of the full price that would be paid if this were to fail. Her eyes searched mine looking for an answer, plastering what I hoped was a convincing smile to my face I gave her one. Even if it wasn't the one, she would need to hear at some point...

"Besides, how often do you get the chance to chastise me?"

Chapter 2

Breakfast's wondrous flavors still lingered on my mind hours later while I sat in the back of a black SUV. Ayi had informed me that this was the way that most wealthy young women would arrive at a shopping mall; I took her word for it. After all she was of this world. I was only used to observing it, and frankly I was still getting use to the wonders of this *new* age.

The bath and dressing portion of the morning revealed that I was slightly different in proportion to Ayi's daughter. While she was willowy and petite, I was curvier yet lean. Though I have yet to use them, my body had well-formed muscles.

Still, my body was soft in all the right places. I thought, a sly smile pulling at my lips. I may have just been transformed into this body, yet, I was no stranger to the effect that the feminine form can have on others. Although the way that these clothes are on me now... My eyes looked down at the clothing I currently wore, and a soft sigh passed over my lips thankfully unnoticed. To say that these clothes were ill fitting would be an understatement. I couldn't wear these garments and meet my soulmate. *No, that would be unacceptable! He would think me a harlot...*

Which is what has brought us here driving down the roadway towards the closest shopping mall. We needed to go shopping and purchase clothing not only for the event-- perhaps something with a hint of the past? No. Hmm, should I try something fun? Something formal? The possibilities were endless, of course I intended to purchase several different outfits.

I found it hard to contain my building excitement. I had never gone shopping before. As a goddess one doesn't need to participate in such trivial activities. If I wanted to wear a particular garment all I needed to do was think about it and it was so. The idea of going shopping was absolutely ridiculous. Or at least that is what I had thought before. Now, however, my mind found it hard to concentrate on what Ayi was saying while she sat next to me explaining the proper way to behave at the shopping district for the second time since we left the estate.

"I will walk behind you, my Lady, as you look over the clothing racks, any articles of clothing you wish to try on I will hold for you until we return to the dressing room. When it is time to check out, umm ... buy the items, I will handle the transaction for you. Nia will carry your purchases back to the car, and..."

"We will return home to the estate, where I will continue my preparations for the night of the thirty-first's event..." Ayi nods a gentle smile on her lips at my response. "I remember your words from before. I will behave as you have instructed, although we will be purchasing many articles of clothing today. I do not wish to have to keep returning to the mall again and again over the coming weeks, unless I must."

"As you wish, my Lady. We are drawing near to our destination..." Ayi's sudden pause made me look over towards her. Her chestnut colored eyes gleamed and a hint of a smile played at her lips. "My Lady..."

"Yes, Ayi?" My voice gave away no hint of the amusement seeing her this way brought me.

"I, well, we; Nia and myself. Have considered your request for assistance with choosing a name. And we believe that Wu Lihwa is a very proper name for you my Lady."

"Wu Lihwa." Wu... that was Xia's surname in 219 BCE and Lihwa means a Princess. The full irony of my newly proposed name wasn't lost on me. After a moment of thought, I nodded my head in agreement, it was after all an accurate description of who and what I am. I am the daughter of a God and Goddess, and therefore would be considered a Princess of sorts.

"Very well, Ayi, get the necessary paperwork done up for my I.D."

Ayi's face brightened at my words. She clapped her hands together once before exclaiming jubilantly. "We already have, my Lady. You asked us over a month ago after all. We just need to get a photo of you, for your ID and Passport. So once you are properly dressed we shall go to the photo booth and get one made." Her eyes twinkled again. A sure sign that she was pleased with her own foresight. "We also have received your degree and diploma in the mail. Your backstory is all in place and 100% verifiable."

I nodded. "Thank you Ayi, you have accomplished much

while I was transitioning and for that I am extremely thankful."

Ayi's face flushed red, before bowing her head in response.

"We have arrived, my Lady, I mean... Wu Lihwa." Nia's cheerful voice carried over the front seats as he pulled the SUV to a stop in front of a large cluster of buildings. Before I could respond to him he hopped out of the vehicle and rounded to the rear door opening it up with the air that he had done this many times before, and not in fact for the very first time ever chauffeuring. With skillful ease he assisted Ayi out of the vehicle before holding out a steady hand for me.

I took Nia's outstretched hand and carefully stepped out of the car. My first true experience out in public, and I didn't want to fall flat on my face. No matter how wobbly my own legs felt.

"Thank you." I whispered taking my first steps towards the door of the closest clothing store, Ayi following a few steps behind.

With a smile curving my lips I approached the door. *Time to see what the clothing world had in store for me.*

§

After several hours of trying on clothing for all occasions I finally decided to wear one of my newly acquired outfits for my photo ID picture. I gazed at my reflection scrutinizing how the fabric clung to my curves, it had long flowing sleeves but bare shoulders. The neckline was modest, yet there was a diamond shaped cutout that showed a little glimpse of my cleavage. It had a traditional floral pattern set into the royal blue background. I chose a pair of black flare cut slacks and wonderful open toed silver wedge heels to complete the ensemble.

Nia's and Ayi's arms were heavy with bags filled with my bounty... Hat boxes and shoe boxes as well as large garment boxes made it difficult for poor Nia to see where he was going.

He only stumbled once as we walked to the car, but to everyone's surprise, including his own, he didn't drop a single thing. We were in desperate need to unload before heading to the photo booth which was clear on the other side of the shopping district, district being the correct terminology I was informed and not mall as I had once thought.

While Nia finished loading the back of the SUV with my purchases, I gazed out over the fascinating scene in front of me. The street was abuzz with people of all ages and classes ambling along chatting. Occasionally they would take the time to stop in front of the elegant window displays, eyeing the mannequin's accessories longingly.

I wondered what it would feel like to have a group of friends shopping with me. Chattering away about clothing and upcoming romantic dates. Is that how Xai Yahui shopped? With a group of his closest friends whiling away the hours? Or does he shop chaperoned, guarded constantly, as I am? My eyes caught the weary gaze of Nia darting around the crowd, ever on the lookout for someone who might intend to harm me. This, I thought, is what he is truly used to. Not driving a car and acting as a butler which I had informed Ayi he would transition into once my transformation was complete. I truly am blessed to have such loyal followers.

"Lihwa... Lihwa, my Lady..." Ayi's breathless voice finally broke my deep concentration, I would really need to get used to being called by that name. "Are you sure that you don't wish to have Nia drive us to the photo booth? It is quite a walk to get there after all."

Sighing I turned placing a smile on my face to hide my disappointment in her suggestion. "Yes, Ayi, I am aware that it is quite a distance away." I paused looking slightly towards the ground before continuing. "I would like to walk it, but..." I let my eyes take in Ayi's breathless expression...she wasn't used to this type of exertion and she wouldn't make the trek across the parking lot again much less the full length of the plaza. "I will go in the SUV if you are unable to traverse so far. I know that you are out of breath and I do apologize for my carelessness and lack of consideration." Bowing my head, once again, I took this opportunity to suggest a solution that I was almost sure I knew the answer to, but it was worth a try, nonetheless. Drawing in a deep breath I gazed up at my loyal caretaker before adding. "I could easily walk there if you would allow me to. You could have Nia drive you over to the booth to meet me there."

Her response was immediate. "No, that is unacceptable. You would be without protection. You must either ride or we both walk. You will not put yourself in any unnecessary danger. Besides you are in no condition to go by yourself."

Ayi's tone was absolute. Again, I bowed my head before walking to the SUV's open back door. Conceding to her for the second time today. *I need to pick my battles wisely.* Trying to contain the laughter that was building up inside me. I added aloud.

"As you wish, Ayi."

Chapter 3

Yahui, what do you think of that one?" Hou Haku's voice called over the bustling crowd of shoppers. Pointing shamelessly at a brunette as she sauntered by with a cluster of guys trailing in her wake.

"You'll never give up will you?" Xai Yahui sighed in frustration. Haku dragged him to the shopping district in hopes of finding a date for him to the New Year's Eve event, seeing's how the girl he was supposed to go with had come down sick.

Thankfully Yahui thought.

Haku, on the other hand, didn't see it as a blessing like Yahui did so they had sat here for the last two hours while Haku pointed out all of the females who walked past them that he found attractive. If he was being honest with himself, most of the girls that Haku pointed out were quite lovely to look at, and they would have made wonderful arm candy for the concert, but they just didn't interest him.

"Haku. I need to go. Let's head back over to the car. Which side did we park near again?"

"Alright, go dateless," he sneered. "For all I care" his voice was barely a mumble while he stared down at the ground between them. Finally shaking his head, he peaked out over a group of passing girls. "Hear me well, Yahui, and remember when all of your female fans start throwing themselves at you on New Year's Eve," Haku turned abruptly, staring at Yahui. Yahui felt the daggers that passed between the two of them before Haku venomously added "Don't come crawling to me for help! You will have to escape them all by yourself, because I won't help you."

"Agreed, I will not go crawling to you begging for help. Now, which way do I need to go to get to the car?"

"We parked over by the photo booth." Haku huffed pointing off to the left..

Yahui nodded pulling his black facemask back over his nose. Securing it into place before he stood up. Being out in public wasn't always a game of intrigue at least before he had become famous, that is. Acting and singing where two occupations he had never considered growing up. He loved to dance. Dancing had always been his dream. But now dancing was only a small part of his performing life, he sighed at that thought, really dancing was only a small part of his life in general now.

Regardless, going out in public alone was generally next to impossible... Unless he went in disguise, and today's disguise had been one of an oversized ragged hoodie, sunglasses, a pair of baggy sweatpants and of course his trusty black facemask, that he never left home without. The effect was that of a poor vagabond, yet it was a small price he was happily willing to pay in order to not have a team of security circling around him everywhere he went.

Not wanting to wait for Haku, Yahui strode out into the walkway, and without even giving a single backwards glance. Yahui made his way through the bustling crowd towards the awaiting car. He couldn't help but think that he should have been back at the auditorium rehearsing all this time instead of wasting two hours here, but he knew that Haku, for all his numerous faults and annoyances, really did have Yahui's best interest at heart, no matter how misguided his attempts were. The concert was five days away, after all, he had plenty of time left to rehearse in the upcoming days.

Weaving through the crowd was easier now than when they first arrived. At first, he thought that maybe it was just less crowded but the truth of the matter was he was much faster because he didn't have to wait for Haku to tag along. Granted he would now have to wait at the car for Haku to arrive, but at least for the short amount of time it would take him to get there, he wouldn't have to listen to Haku's running commentary on the females that they would pass on their way.

Yahui shook his head, knowing full well he would have to listen to Haku's continuing barrage of complaints once they were both in the car. But to be honest, Yahui couldn't find it in himself to actually care at this point, as long as right now he got to the car in a semi peaceful manner.

Rounding the last corner before the photo booth Yahui slowed his pace. The glint of the early afternoon sun from a shiny Black SUV with dark tinted windows pulling to a stop made him come to a complete halt. Especially when he noticed that the SUV's driver jumped out rushing around to open the rear passenger side door. A slight smile pulled at the corner of his lips, *so he wasn't the only celebrity here after all*. Curiosity might kill the cat, but what could it hurt to see who this new arrival was.

Yahui dashed closer to a pillar a short distance from the photo booth. A perfect vantage point to watch from and see just who had arrived. It's probably someone who he knew already, after all, but... Glancing down at his attire he thought that he probably should wait until they are completely out of sight before heading to the car. Just in case...

An elegant older lady with silver hair tucked into a knot stepped out of the SUV first. She moved with grace as she stepped aside turning back towards the open door.

It was only a second, maybe two, though it could have been a lifetime, before a long slender hand reached from the darkness to grab hold of the driver's outstretched one. . An open toed silver shoe stepped onto the pavement just moments before a sudden burst of wind blew long flowing Chestnut and honey strands of hair up into the air. A mesmerizing halo framing the most angelic face he had ever seen.

Yahui sucked in a large breath holding it while he watched her push back a lock of hair from her face. Her amber eyes shone bright catching the sun's light, they may have been more than three meters apart, yet he could see her beautiful eyes as if he was standing directly in front of her. A long-forgotten memory pulled at him. *Those eyes.*

"Yahui, there you are, the car is over here... I guess I can forgive you for leaving me behind seeing as you at least stopped here... Are you hiding from someone? Or..." Haku's voice trailed off... "Wow!!! Yahui, now I see why you stopped here..." Haku jabbed his elbow sharply into Yahui's side... "So, how about that one?"

"Yes," Yahui replied instantly blowing out his held breath. "Most definitely. Yes!"

"So... I'll just go up to her and ask ..."

Yahui grabbed Haku's arm before he could even take a step. "No. You're not doing anything." he hissed. Watching as this unknown vision of loveliness walked to the photo booth. Stopping before the curtain she waited until her silver haired escort opened it for her before entering. Taking this as the most opportune moment Yahui pulled off his mask, threw back the hood and stuffed his sunglasses into his pocket before he walked up to her escort, bowing low once he was standing fully in front of her.

"Hello, Madam, you may not know me, but my name is--"

A hysterical scream sounded from a good distance behind him, too close for his liking. "Oh my God! It's Xai Yahui!" Cringing slightly, Yahui peered quickly over his shoulder before turning his attention back to the woman before him.

"Sorry, my name is Xai Yahui, and I would like to ask permission to meet your Lady and invite her out as my date to the New Year's Countdown Concert, it seems that the meeting part might have to wait." reaching into his pocket he pulled out a business card and handed it to the lady before him. She received it gracefully with two hands. The sound of female screams grew louder, and he could only guess that he had only a matter of seconds before the amassing crowd of fans would be on them. "here is my card, if your lady is willing to accept my offer she can call this number and we can make all the proper arrangements... and a time to pick her up." He lowered his head before adding "Thank you, please excuse me."

The words were barely out of his mouth before Yahui's arm was pulled from behind him. Haku half dragged half pulled Yahui towards the parking lot. They had just made it to the row that the car was on before Haku spoke in short spurts. "Not the best... introduction you've ever given...but hopefully you'll hear from her." With the car before them Haku pulled the car keys from his pocket, pressing the unlock button multiple times hurriedly before they heard the familiar clicking sound letting them know that the doors were in fact unlocked. Releasing his hold on Yahui's arm. Haku rounded to the driver's side door. "Now get in the car. You lucky dog."

"I'll only be lucky if she responds." Yahui's lips curled into a hopeful smile before jumping into the bucket seats of Haku's vintage sports car.

Chapter 4

Ayi held the card out toward the opening in the curtain while I watched Xai Yahui runaway with a large group of fans giving chase. Taking the card into my hands I smiled pressing the small rectangle of sturdy paper to my lips. A bubble of giggles formed in my chest from the irony of it all. I had known, without a shadow of a doubt, that New Year's night was important, after all I had glimpses of a vision allowing me some knowledge of that fact. But I had never envisioned that this would be the way that things would unfold. *And to think I would have missed him had I walked instead of taking the SUV.*

"Your photos are ready, my Lady. We must return to the house in order for you to continue your preparations." Ayi tucked the freshly printed photos into her handbag, patiently waiting for my response.

"Yes, Ayi. Thank you." My legs moved automatically at a slow and steady pace, it took all of my restraint to keep myself from running to the vehicle just so I could call the number that was printed on the card that I had pressed firmly over my heart... It wasn't until I reached the SUV that I remembered that I had a major flaw in my plan. Sliding into the backseat of the SUV I waited until Nia closed the door behind Ayi. Before I addressed this major issue.

My heart was hammering in my chest all the while that the words poured out of me.

"Ayi, I don't have a phone. I need you to please get me one." my voice broke, sounding like a schoolgirl asking for a new toy, instead of a grown woman requesting a necessary tool.

"At once my Lady." Ayi nodded her hand fumbling around with a stack of boxes that rested on the floorboard by her feet. Grabbing three of the boxes she pulled them out offering them to me with that glitter in her eye. "Which one would my Lady like. We bought you three."

§

I waited until I arrived back at my home before I attempted to call him. Battling with these newfound feelings that have come over me, Ayi called them nerves. I called them annoyances, for I shook so badly my fingers fumbled on the touchscreen above the numbers. Finally, after thirty minutes of failed attempts and many wrong numbers, the phone rang once, twice, and then on the third ring I heard the unmistakable sound of Yahui's voice.

"Hello?"

My body quivered uncontrollably, I finally forced myself to respond. "Hello...Xai Yahui?" I took a deep calming breath although it did nothing for my nerves. I am sure that I heard a noise that I took as affirmation. I needed to give him my response. Blowing my breath out slowly I continued. "My answer to your request is yes. I will give the phone to my caretaker, Ayi, and she will make all the necessary arrangements along with giving you directions to my estate."

I couldn't even hold the phone long enough to hear his reply before, with trembling hands, I passed the phone off to Ayi. It was awful. I couldn't even listen to Yahui's response, my mind was a flutter. What is this feeling? Do all humans feel like this when they first talk to the person that they love? I knew Yahui, I knew his soule and the lives that he had lived over the millennia... Why than is every fiber of my being jumping like tiny sparks in a flame?

Wrapping my arms around my legs I pulled my knees to my chest. Willing my body to stop its unrelenting trembling. I closed my eyes in a desperate attempt to calm myself even more, picturing the calm still waters of the pond outside. I told myself to relax; for all the good that was.

The feelings of love that I had while being a higher being where nothing in comparison to these. I knew that the world felt new when I was with him in ethereal form all those years ago. But this feeling that had taken over my whole body was something quite different. We haven't even truly met... Yet I knew that this was it. This was the moment that would decide my fate and his for that matter. This will change the remainder of my life. How could it not be one that would set my nerves to jumping? Why would it not make my heart race, my face blush? Why wouldn't his name be the only one that I wanted to hear for the remainder of eternity?

Lost in my thoughts I was completely unaware of everything around me until the sound of Ayi's voice brought me

[33]

back to myself...

"My Lady? Are you alright?" Ayi's light touch landed on my shoulder. Gently reminding me that I was truly here.

"Yes," I sighed "Yes perfectly fine. What did he say?" Standing quickly before her I let my eyes search hers. Longing to grasp the knowledge that she had, and I desperately needed.

Ayi laughed softly before she took my hands into hers. "My dear goddess, he says, that it's a casual affair. No need to dress in formal attire. He will be wearing a silver and black jeweled sweater with black jeans and shoes. He also was hoping that you might dress to match. I wonder..." she paused... "Didn't you purchase such an outfit today my Lady?" She paused again this time looking at me with an awed expression... I nodded with a smile pulling on my lips, I lifted two fingers into the air. She continued "Ahh yes, two such outfits. Of course, you knew. Anyways, because it will be a long night he respectfully asked permission to keep you out past midnight, it will be a New Year's celebration after all. I told him my Lady will be able to stay out if that is what she wishes."

A squeal of delight erupted out of me while I latched on to Ayi's surprised body and hugged her tightly to me.

"My Lady, you need to make yourself presentable, he made reference to sending you something this afternoon... And I wouldn't be surprised if he accompanied the gift himself."

"Oh Ayi, he would be gift enough. But I will go and get ready" I could feel my cheeks flushing. "Thank you, Ayi!" I kissed her cheek, grabbing the phone from her hand before I raced down the long corridor towards my bedroom, anxious to get ready.

The clock on the wall showed it was already two o'clock. I wondered how long it would take to have a gift delivered. The answer to my question was given in short order: not long at all... it was three thirty when the sound of tires crushing gravel made me race to the doorway. Anxiously awaiting the knock that would announce the arrival of my love's gift...

Nia opened the door on the first knock... everyone in the estate had been alerted to the arrival by my exuberant dash to the foray... If I hadn't been on high alert Nia would have taken longer to answer the door.

Once open we were greeted by a beautiful bouquet of flowers from roses to carnations with an iris thrown in to boot. With my love for everything botanical, I smiled at the vast array of meanings just that bouquet alone represented.

If that had been all that was in the arms of the man at the door- it would have been sufficient, but once Nia took the flowers there was two boxes there one a rather large rectangular box with several different photos all showing people using a piece of electronics, the other was smaller but looked to be of an electronic nature as well.

Unable to stay in my hiding place any longer I found my feet carrying me closer to the man at the door. He remained hidden behind the boxes in his arms, but I knew who it was: for every fiber of my being were screaming that this was Yahui. It was my love.

Still I played along, wondering what the gifts could possibly be.

"What lovely flowers. Are they for me?" I let my singsong voice carry over the entrance making sure that Yahui could hear every word.

"There is a card my Lady." Nia's smile beamed on his youthful face. With bated breath I watched Yahui's body go rigid. To my chagrin with each step I took closer I noticed him trying

[35]

to sneak a peek from behind the boxes.

"Yes, I see there is... Thank you..." I took the card in both hands before leaning in to inhale the wonderful fragrances of the flowers.

"Ayi, would you be kind enough to place these flowers into a Vase for me. And please Nia, invite our guest to come in and unburdened himself of his packages. They look to be quite bulky and cumbersome." I smiled opening the envelope that held the card. "Ayi, please bring some milk tea for our dutiful delivery man."

"Of course my lady." Ayi turned and left with the bouquet in her arms.

Try as I might, I could not stop my hands from shaking ever so slightly while I began to read the enclosed note.

> 'To the lady who holds all the cards. I fear that I have yet to learn your name. Regardless of that fact, these flowers pale in comparison to your beauty. Please accept these offerings as my appreciation of your acceptance to my sudden request for a date New Year's Eve evening.
>   Your humble servant,
>   Xai Yahui'

I could feel my cheeks burn from the sweet words. I needed to be careful in my response. Turning I watched Yahui stroll up to a long table to set down the boxes that he held in his arms. He wore form fitting blue jeans and a white dress shirt. A far cry from the sweatpants and hoodie I had seen him in only a few hours ago. His dark brown hair was tousled so handsomely one would think that he had spent hours styling it. Yahui, his arms now empty, turned slowly and with deliberate purpose to face me. His caramel brown eyes found mine and his mouth parted slightly while he let his eyes take me all in. I hadn't bothered to change my clothes; however, I did take my hair down, smoothed out and straightened with a straightening iron. The effect had been that my hair shined in the artificial light of the foray's chandelier.

After a moment he seemed to notice that he was staring, and he let his eyes lower to the floor. I smiled biting my lip trying as hard as I could not to mention the awkward tension that hung between us.

Making my way to the packages that he had placed on the table. I was able to better see what he had brought. One held a gaming laptop and another, much smaller box, had a wireless headset with retractable microphone. A vision passed before me, a memory really, of when I was watching Yahui playing on a system similar to this. Although, I must admit that I have never once attempted to use one. Not even when I was at the Academy.

The gifts touched my heart thoroughly. For it was another side of Yahui that he was attempting to include me in.

"Xai Yahui... I am honored by your wonderful gifts. However, I must insist that your offerings are too great. I cannot accept them." I bowed my head low to him.

"No, my Lady. I insist that you accept these humble gifts as a token of my good intentions. I failed to introduce myself properly in the shopping district. So please forgive my boldness in delivering these to you now, in person. Even going as far to hide my identity from you for as long as I could." His face grew red. Pausing he took a deep breath before he continued. "You have shown me in your actions the merit of your true character. In the

[37]

way that you open your home to even someone you thought was a delivery employee." He bowed and then moved to stand next to me. "Please accept these trinkets. Has the Lady ever played Online?"

I smiled meekly before shaking my head no.

"If the Lady would like I would be honored to show her how." His face was lit with joy and I was taken in by the innocence of his grin. A smile was etching itself onto my lips. The feelings I was having so new yet also not completely foreign to me... I was fully aware of what they meant. Inhaling deeply through my nose I began to open my mouth to respond, but before my lips even parted a loud excessive blaring of a car horn sounded from the driveway.

Yahui rolled his eyes and clenched his fists tightly into balls. "Please excuse my impatient friend. I best head out before he decides to honk again. Ummm. Do you have a piece of paper and something to write with? I will jot down a website and my username so that we can meet up online later. If you want to, that is..."

I gave a curt nod and his eyes beamed to match his full grin. I went to the table that the boxes were sitting on. Pulling out a piece of paper and pen from the table's center drawer, then turning I held them out to him. Yahui smile brought more heat to my face. Our hands briefly touched as he took the items from me. Without another word he bent over the table scribbling a few words, letters, symbols, and numbers onto the page. Once finished he stood placing the pen down onto the table.

His eyes met mine, his lips parting as his eyes searched mine long fully... He made to step forward his foot hung in the air for a moment, stopping as quickly as he had started, he placed his foot back down on the floor; then he spoke.

"I look forward to seeing you soon online. Until then..."
he bowed his head, then with a fluid motion he stood up before
turning towards the door to leave. Nia opened the door for him
to exit. Swiftly as I could I strode evenly with him, matching his
pace with my own to the doorway. Once outside I watched him
run to the blue sedan that was sitting in the driveway with the
motor running. A familiar looking man sat behind the steering
wheel. Try as I may, I just couldn't place from whence I had seen
him before.

Leaning my head against the doorframe I continued to
watch until the sedan was totally out of sight, before closing the
door and racing over to my new gifts.

"Nia, I will need your assistance. We need to get this set up
and me online before anything else gets done this evening."

Chapter 5

It took Nia and I a full hour to get the laptop set up and registered. Not to mention the update installed. Then we had to download the game that Yahui indicated and make myself a character. My attention was fully on the game. I was so intrigued that I even played through all the tutorial missions before I did a search for Yahui's Username GuYan9991, the name came up and a small green light indicated that he was in fact online.

Smiling I typed each letter slowly into the message box that Nia had opened for me. It was time to send him my own username: WeiYong and to thank him again for his presents, and his thoughtfulness. Pushing send I let my eyes roam over the screen. A loud dinging sound rang in my ear, alerting me of a message.

Yahui had responded nearly at once. He gave instructions on how to add him to an actual live chat. After clicking on a few places, I heard Yahui's voice in my ears. A slight shiver ran down my spine in response.

"Hello... I'm sending you a friend request. Oh, wait what level are you at?" I smiled before replying. The tutorials had certainly paid off. I was able to level up quite quickly.

With satisfaction ringing in my voice I gave my response. "Thirteen."

"Wow. You have been busy. That is perfect." I could hear the clicking of keys on the other end... "There...Friend request sent."

Ayi shook her head as she walked behind my seat at the long dining room table, I had made into my gaming room desk. Yahui's voice came over the earphones in a gentle tone.

"Wei Yong, I like it, is that your name? Seeing how I once again forgot to ask you for yours before having to run off."

"I do see where that has been a thing for you... Should I be worried?" a small chuckle flowed from my lips... "And if you have forgotten to ask me for my name twice now, just how important could it be to you? You can call me Wei Yong... although, it is not my real name. Perhaps, if you are lucky, I will give you my true name New Year's Eve evening." I laughed again a full belly laugh that made my side ache... "But then again, I might not."

A mischievous grin toyed at my lips. The silence on the other end made my smile even wider. Satisfied for now, I began looking at the long list of 'skins' that were available for my character. I had chosen to be a female warrior instead of the winged elf, both had their positive points I suppose. But I had the need to be stronger, able to fight and protect, and this warrior seemed to be the perfect solution to that need...

Pangu, is the digitally designed world our characters are in, it was strangely familiar... but no matter how hard I tried I wasn't able to place my finger on to exactly where I had seen or heard of it before. Letting go of that thought for now I started to go through the long list of 'skins' again. I found several outfits that I liked very much and many that were absolutely horrible. The prices on these items were outrageous. My poor new warrior didn't have nearly enough to even think of buying the semi-decent skin, never mind trying to even look at the more expensive ones.

"Gu Yan how do I obtain the adequate funds to purchase these skins? I see an outfit that I really like."

"Well that depends on the outfit... some you cannot purchase but have to earn by doing quests. Which can take a while, while others you can earn and/or collect gold to purchase the items. There is another way but..." There was a slight pause and at first I thought that maybe we had lost each other. I checked my computer screen frantically not seeing any indications that we had lost connection, and he still appeared to be online. My nerves were put at ease a moment later.... "Which outfit are you looking at?"

I sighed collecting myself before responding. "The Mandarin silk one, it is really quite lovely."

"Yes, that is a nice one. I think that I could help you power through the levels in order to get that. You have to be a level thirty to even buy it...and you are just barely a level thirteen correct?" He paused, yet I didn't have time to even respond before he continued.

"It may involve a lot of grinding, but I think we can get you into that outfit before the end of the night if you wanna put in the time."

"Grinding?" My face blushed. "Ummm...that sounds like something that I shouldn't be doing." A nervous laugh escaped my lips while my face flooded with even more heat. The silence on the other end made me even more anxious for a moment. A heartbeat maybe two later Yahui's voice purred into my ear.

"I think that you would be able to do the grinding in this context, Wei Yong... You've never gamed before have you? I mean I know that you haven't gamed online before... But..."

By the gods how do humans stand these emotions...I absentmindedly fanned my face with my hands... in an attempt to help the flaming heat from my face calm down..."No, Gu Yan, this is my first time. So please be gentle with me."

Yahui coughed before there was silence again.

"Gu Yan? Are you still there?"

"Yes. I just had to mute my mic for a moment... or I would have hurt your ears laughing."

Mute mic... hmmm... mute to silence... "You can do that, this muting of the mic?"

"Yes, on the side of your headset there is a number of controls, one of them will allow you to mute the mic. Also, before you ask, no, I wasn't laughing at you but laughing at what my mind thought when you said to be gentle. Please forgive me."

Forgive him? That was an easy request, I already had. And always will...but would he forgive me...? I already knew that I was going to be in trouble if I didn't start toning my hormones down a few notches. For some reason it was all too easy to say the first things that came to my mind... No filtration... Perhaps it was because I was wielding these computer-generated swords. Or maybe, it was the fact that I was here safe in my own surroundings and I need not worry so much. Either way, I could start to really see why so many people lose themselves in these gaming worlds.

I felt so powerful and free.

That being said... it didn't fully explain why my emotions where all over the place. Was this normal for a human? Is this what I will have to deal with for as long as I live? Ayi didn't seem to be afflicted with this problem... I felt so much like a naive and giddy little schoolgirl. I could only hope that Yahui would not think I wasn't worthy of his time. Nor of his love....

§

After several hours of 'grinding' and ten level ups later we entered into a city ... Grinding, it turned out, is what you do when you continuously battle to increase your 'experience points (EXP)' and also your 'in game gold'. Yahui said that there was a guild that had numerous quests posted in this city. Hence the reason we traveled here. I was totally enthralled with the excitement of the game. Not to mention the time I was spending chatting with Yahui.

Looking at my screen I had to admire the ability of the game designer to make a city appear so similar to that of past civilizations. My eyes took in the depths of the landscapes, the towering marketplace pavilions and well-defined horizons. Several multicolored flags flapped in the... well, in what I could only call a breeze. Though I felt none coming from the screen.

How unusual this virtual world was. The attention to detail from the soft stones that lined the narrow streets to the way that the shadows cast their darkened "reflection" onto the ground and their other surroundings. Yahui and I were here in Pangu still, of course, but now in the city of Nye. Yet, when you think about it, we weren't really here at all. It reminds me of how I was able to attend the Academy in Paris, France.

My mind raced with the memory. When I attended the

academy, I was there but I wasn't in a true human form. Not really. Nothing like how I was now anyway... I looked and sounded like the group of people around me. I even had adopted a *willowy* appearance. Slender yet strong. *Easy on the eyes*, Nia once told me. I had to take his word for it... When I looked at myself in the mirror all I saw was my true ethereal form. Nevertheless, I was solid, but I couldn't taste, I could touch but I couldn't feel...I could smell but I couldn't truly differentiate between the scents. All my male dance partners would tell me how very light I was, so easy to lift that they would argue over who would partner with me on lift days.

Now, well now I can experience all the richness's of tastes, scents, and touch that are truly available. I can eat and enjoy the flavors, like the mint water that I was now drinking, thanks to Ayi's ever watchful eyes. I thought as I brought the cold glass to my lips again, inhaling the aroma of the mint, tasting its freshness with each sip.

Although those inabilities were only small annoyances, in reality there was only one huge downside in the life of a goddess making herself appear visible to humans. I couldn't... Well, I couldn't stay in that form for very long. After an eight-hour day of classes I would need to transform back into my ethereal form. I suppose it wasn't all that bad of a thing. Seeing as I would be able to take in the world around me in a totally different way than my fellow classmates.

I learned so much during that time. Obtaining as much information about the drastically different world. So much had changed since the time I went into my immortal slumber. I had to learn the nuances of this time. Or else when I did become human, I wouldn't be able to fit in. An outcast. A freak.

On days when I had no classes, while in my corporeal

form, I spent my free time in the Library touching each book in turn along the many shelves. While my classmates were locked away in their rooms hunched over their textbooks that they were reading for homework over and over again studying away. I was acquiring the required information and so much more just by placing my finger on the spine of the books. What was taking them hours I was doing in seconds.

If they only knew... A slight chuckle passed my lips. The vibration of air and sound was easily caught then amplified by the tiny mic that was only a few centimeters from my lips.

I felt the vibrations of sound pulse through the headphones as Yahui's mirthful laughter travel the distance from his home to me. "Wei Yong?" his alluring deep tones flowed through the headset tickling my ears bringing me out of my musings. "What is so funny?"

"Oh... Well I was just remembering when I was in Paris."

"Really? Paris? Are you going to share? Or should I guess... hmmm what could it be that you found so humorous?"

A burst of air past over my lips again. This time more undeniably. The first time I hadn't meant to laugh, out loud at least, this time I most certainly did. "You will have to keep guessing..." A playful smile pulled at my moist lips. "I will not reveal my deepest thoughts to you so freely... I mean, what will I get in return for such a revealing truth? Will you tell me what you are thinking? Perhaps, what you were thinking about back when you muted your mic?"

Before he could respond a flash of light caught my attention. My eyes scanned the screen looking for the cause. The screen was covered with what Yahui had called icons. There was Icons with numerous shapes ones that looked like swords for battling, one that looked like a shield for blocking, and another that has a small satchel on it representing all of the items that you are holding. But none of them looked any different than they had a moment ago, before the flash of light that is.

At the bottom of the screen was a small box with text scrolling by. Yahui had explained that this was the message box that would show a brief display of what was going on in the game. Conversations with other players, and much more... It was like a language all their own, and it fascinated me to no end. Still there was nothing there that would indicate what the cause of the flash was.

Traveling further left I noticed a little exclamation mark hovering near a small icon of a scroll. I couldn't remember seeing it before...

"Sooo... Did you get the quest?" Yahui's voice resonated in the headset...

"Ah, is that what the scroll is... A quest. If so then, Yes, I did receive it." I moved my curser over the icon, a small text box popped up.

"That's great, now click it and except the quest and I will take it from there."

"Oh... okay..." I did as he asked clicking the icon's bold text which gave the name of the quest: The Dragon Hunter.

"Because we have already partnered up in a party your character should automatically follow mine."

"Okay..." Sure enough after clicking on the except button it was just like he said, my character started moving without my assistance, matching the direction of Yahui's.

"B.T.W... I would answer any questions about myself that you wanted to know. But I can understand that I might be being too forward here. It is easy to lose yourself in the game. And the relationships here are so unlike that of the relationships that you have I.R.L...."

B.T.W.? I.R.L.? I let my mind race. Trying to find the relevant information to help me understand. I thought back to my time at the academy and once again let my mind traipse through the vast amount of information that I had obtained. *B.T.W...* I know that I had heard that said or had seen it written before. *Oh,* the memory hit me in flashes. Text messages on phones from fellow students to each other in the hallways between classes. B.T.W. equals *By the way...* But I don't recall what I.R.L. was. It must be unique to these gaming worlds.

I knew that if I wanted to know what it was, I would need to ask. No matter how much I loathed to admit it. My fingers couldn't gain the information for me this time.

"Ya..." I started about to call him by his true name. Something he expressly told me you do not do. "Um... Gu Yan, what does *I. R. L.* mean?" My voice wavered, even to my own ears, I sounded like an unsure mouse, instead of a supposedly all-knowing goddess.

A light chiming of a laugh once again resonated in the headset. "Sorry, Wei Yong, you have been playing so well that I forgot that you have never chatted in game... or online with anyone in these contexts. I.R.L. means in real life. Please, if I say anything else that you don't understand feel free to ask me."

In real life... I felt a tightening in my chest. In real life... That is what I was doing. Living a life. No matter how fleeting it may turn out to be.

"Thank you, Gu Yan. I will."

The screen flashed again this time a mythical Dragon emerged, it's glowing blue scales and red eyes bursting onto the screen. Filling it from one edged the screen to the other. Then it dropped back into the background so that our battle-ready warriors could engage in the fray. Once again, I took control of my character. Clicking on the icons to make her fight: lunging and parrying to the best of my ability that is.

My hits were like "love taps." Yahui had told me. But, they would grow stronger. I wanted them to. I needed them to. I needed to be as strong in the game as he was if not stronger. It was irrational, I know, but the need to be able to protect him out-weighed everything else. I watched as every hit Yahui's character struck greatly reduced the hit points of the quest boss. While mine were mere pokes, his were mighty blows. It was amazing to watch.

It was like watching his past lives fight in times of war... where instead of winning great rewards and treasures, they were fighting for their lives as well as their lord's commands.

This time's Yahui is still very much a warrior... I smiled admiring the way that he controlled his character so effortlessly. While I stumbled over the keys. His fingers were dancing with precision. I sighed inwardly, missing the godly ability I used so often in Academy. These fingers of bone and flesh could not gain the knowledge that I desired. (I did not know if I would ever regain any of my powers.) But regardless my fingers could be trained. With time... To dance along the keyboard much like Yahui's were doing right now.

Chapter 6

The light from the bedside lamp illuminated not only the room, but Yahui's newest script as well. He was unable to sleep, having just finished up playing online with Wei Yong... His mind refused to focus on anything other than the woman who, ever since he saw her exiting her SUV yesterday, has been in the forefront of his mind. He couldn't help but feel that he knew her. No. It was more than that... He felt like his whole being belonged with her.

"Good thought, dumb ass..." Yahui scrubbed his exhausted face with his hands combing through his hair. "You are really gonna impress her with that line!" But the truth was he didn't understand these feelings at all.

Tossing the script down onto the floor Yahui ambled out of his bedroom down the hallway towards his office. Forty five steps later he was sitting at his computer and entering back into the game. When they had said goodnight, they had almost accumulated enough gold for her to purchase the skin that she wanted. She had already surpassed the required level of thirty by leaps and bounds.

A smile played on his lips as he remembered her words once she hit that milestone: 'Holy Parents of Me'! He was sure that she wasn't used to cussing. And even those words she was weary saying judging by the prolonged silence post remark. Yet the part that he wished he had been there to watch was just moments after that. He could almost picture her sitting there playing the game when she realized that she couldn't yet purchase her much wanted skin. He smiled. That would have been a treat to watch...

Had Jang not been in such a hurry to leave he would have been able to spend more physical time with her. Helping her set up the laptop would have been a real treat. But nonetheless they had spent nearly ten hours playing together.

"And she promised to log-in this evening as well." He sighed looking at the screen shots he had taken of their avatars. "I wish I had suggested a time sooner than five pm now." He chastised himself. But she needs to get some sleep. And truth be told so did he.

Returning to the main screen he looked at the world map. He had to think of someplace nice in game to take her. No matter how long he thought on the matter, nor how many times he went through the world maps index, there was only one area that met all those requirements: The Lou Hang Canyon. She had just broken the level fifty mark before going to bed, and she needed to gain ten more levels before she could go there. He clicked on their friendship screen and to his surprise saw that she was still online.

Frantically he removed his wireless headset from its charging station, his hands fumbling with them all the while that he was pulling them over his head to rest on his ears. Finally once they were in position he let her in game name, not to mention the fact that it was the only name he knew her by, slip over his lips...

"Wei Yong, I wasn't expecting to see you online...." No matter how much he was hoping to hear her melodic tones. He was instantly met by the heart deflating sound of silence. "She must've forgotten to log out." Laughing out loud, he silently acknowledged that she probably doesn't even know how to properly sign out.

Had this been anyone else besides her those words and thoughts would've been ridiculous. Yet he knew these simple truths to be real. Wei Yong had no prior gaming experience, none. Not even on a console she had confessed... and yet she was gaining levels and skills at an awe inspiring rate... She is an extremely fast study, and that just made his regard for her that much stronger.

"Urg" he growled once again rubbing his hands over his face. Leaning back in defeat, the only good thing was the feel of the soft leather gaming chair that cradled him in comfort. *Money well spent.* He thought as his eyes scanned the screen taking in all the pertinent information...

Everything was there, her EXP was fantastic for someone who just started the game. Her attributes were well distributed. He didn't even have to show her how to do that. Grudgingly she had decided that she needed to spend some of her coveted gold to upgrade her weapons... An excellent choice seeing how her other sword had kept breaking and needing repairs. A sly crooked smile spread over his lips once he had looked at the status of their party.

"She forgot to sign off." He muttered sitting up straight, his right hand moving the wireless mouse over the mousepad. Causing his character to move in a circle. His smile grew broader still as not two steps behind, fallowing in that same circular path, was Wei Yong's avatar...

"Perfect!" Yahui's voice echoing throughout the silent house. "Lou Hang Canyon here we come."

§

The appointed hour was drawing near. Yahui played all morning long only after reaching level sixty with her character had he placed them both into offline botting. He figured he had slept for about three hours by the time his alarm went off at four. Enough time to eat, shower, restock his little refrigerator with drinks and snacks... Not to mention hitting up the restroom before it was time to log back on.

Or at least it should have taken him that long. But today he was finding that time was dragging on and on. He had completed all his tasks and still he was positioned in front of the computer at four twenty-eight.

Before going to bed he had sent Wei Yong an invite to join him at Lou Hang Canyon when she logged on. Had he not been a coward he would have sent her a text to see if maybe she wanted to meet up early. He had her number after all. Or at least he believed that was her number she had called him with.

Picking up his phone he noticed he had multiple messages waiting for him. Haku, of course, was the majority of the thirty-three text messages that his notification screen was filled with. Twenty-nine of them being just from him. Haku could wait, Yahui wasn't in the mood to rehash everything with his good friend and manager. At least not at this moment... He had one message from his mom, her normal once a day check in. He quickly sent off a short response to her before she called the police to come and check up on him. Leaving three messages from a number that he wasn't completely familiar with, yet it looked like a number he should know...

12:32pm

Yahui... I see that my Character has gained levels while I slept. Is this normal?

12:45pm

Yahui... I was wondering... how do I get to Lou Hang Canyon?

3:25pm

I hope that you are alright... I haven't found you online. I know that you said five but... Anyways. Ayi said I am being impatient. I told her that I wasn't... I am just anxious to show you what I did in game... I guess you are either busy or sleeping...I will see you at five.

All this time he had been worried that he would seem to forward if he texted her. And here she was not afraid to send the first ones.

Without further delay he placed his headset on and waited, impatiently, as the log in screen finished loading. Once he was logged in, he checked his message box and sure enough he had several from Wei Yong. He should have taken the time to read them, he knew but decided to wait until he was at Lou Hang Canyon... Opening up the map, Yahui chose the fast travel icon to bring him there.

Upon arrival he was met by a breathtaking sight. A woman sat beneath the blooming cherry tree looking out over the mystical landscape. Her long black hair cascading down over her red silk dress. Cherry blossom petals lay scattered around her some of them had even landed softly on top of her head. He at once felt a pang of guilt for making her wait so long, as well as being overwhelmed by the beauty of this scene.

He wasn't just talking about the outcropping of plateaus that appeared to be floating in the low hanging clouds either.

"This place is absolutely beautiful, Gu Yan." Wei Yong's voice echoed through his headset.

"Mm hmm..." Yahui agreed his eyes only looking at her avatar.

He could picture the real 'Wei Yong' sitting beneath the cherry tree. Her long flowing hair dancing around her in the breeze... In his vision, she turned her head, her eyes were closed but her lips were pulled up into the most beautiful smile.

He stepped closer closing the distance. Feeling that he was way too far away from this vision of loveliness. Once he was within arm's reach of her she opened her eyes and gazed up at him... Her eyes... they are so beautiful... They were the same color as the falling cherry blossom petals. She looked like a goddess. A radiant glow engulfing her. He opened his mouth to speak, but he couldn't... he couldn't find the adequate words to describe his feelings.

She was the one.

The one from his dreams.

And her name is...

Urg... he couldn't say it ... He knew it, just as sure as he knew his own name. He knew her name in the depths of his very being... Dumbstruck he sat there, not even blinking as he stared at the screen... The waking dream had faded but the scene was still playing out in front of him... Wei Yong... No that isn't her name...

"Gu Yan? Are you alright? Gu Yan!?!"

Yahui blinked several times before he forced himself to speak. Looking anywhere but at the screen.

"Yes, Wei Yong, I am fine. I just had to be AFK for a minute..."

"AFK?" her soft musical tones sent warm tingles all over him, like he was standing in the sunlight on a summer's day and a soft warm breeze had tickled his flesh. "What does that mean?"

Yahui felt his lips curl into his trademark grin before he laughed slightly.

"Wei Yong, AFK means away from keyboard."

"Are you laughing at me? Gu Yan?"

"No... Not at you. I only chuckled because I think it is so... Hmmm how can I say this without you getting mad at me..."

Should I say cute? Or is that to childlike. She is not a child, nor do I want here to think that I view her that way. I can't say sweet, can I? Urggg... All the relationships that he had had in his life hadn't prepared him for this. For this was something totally different.

"I think that the way that you question this gaming world around you and the terms that are used here every day is absolutely and totally delightful. Not to mention extremely endearing."

"Well then I will endeavor to continue my pursuit of knowledge." Her voice purred once again. Sounding like the wind chimes that are at the temples in the mountains. Sweetly lulling him into her warm embrace...

Wow... Slow down you idiot, she just has an incredibly attractive voice. That just so happens to belong to an incredibly beautiful young lady. Yahui let his eyes roam over the scene on his computer screen once again. It was apparent that she had obtained the gold needed to purchase the skin, and a new hair style or is that how her avatar transforms when entering this area.

He knew his character had dawned a more leisure attire, as this was a battle free zone.

"I really like your new skin... And did you buy a new hair style as well?"

Her responding giggle brought a smile to his lips once again a pleasant tingling traveled over him. "The skin yes, the hair just kind of appeared like this when I entered this area. BTW it is beautiful here. I did a little online research..."

Huh, she is even incorporating what she learned yesterday already into her chatting... "Oh and what is it that you looked up?"

"I looked up Lou Hang Canyon... Did you know that this place is considered the top spot for couples in this game?"

"You don't say...?" Yahui said leaning back into the soft leather of his chair, relaxing after making his avatar sit down next to Wei Yong's. "Do you not want to be here with me?"

"I never said that..." Her voice rose an octave in response to his question. "I was just wondering what you were expecting of me Gu Yan. As it is, we have only met a little over twenty-four hours ago."

"Expecting from you? My dear Lady, I expect nothing. My only wish is to get to know you better."

"But all of the articles online clearly state that after a certain amount of time here in this area together that an option to purpose will become available..." her voice had softened and became as meek as it had the first time she had asked him what IRL meant.

Yahui leaned forward once again looking at Wei Yong's avatar much like he would her if she was sitting here with him.

"My Lady, I mean no disrespect. In games such as these, perfect strangers have begun in game relations much quicker than we have. Some will even start a conversation by asking if you want to get married." He heard a sharp intake of air through his headset. "But I want to get to know you... Wei Yong. We already have a date IRL looming before us. And I thought that we could spend time together here, or anywhere else in game if you so wish, doing just that."

Yahui waited. It seemed like an eternity before he felt the vibrations of sound coming from her, carrying the sweetest sound and the greatest joy from three tiny words...

"So do I."

Chapter 7

The bright sunlight filtered in through my open curtains. Shining directly onto my face. Yet, I was sure that it must be too early for the sun to be in this position. Yahui and I had played the computer game until the wee hours of the morning. Something that we had done each night since I had awakened... But last night I didn't come to bed until Ayi threatened to turn off the power, I think that was around four a.m.

While it wasn't conventional dating. I had learned a lot more about Yahui and about myself these last four days. For example, I learned that I am pretty good at fighting... at least in the computer generated world. I giggled, But oh the way that Yahui and I spoke with each other had my heart feeling like it was going to explode from pure bliss.

I let my eye's flitter to the clock that hung on the wall above the vanity and nearly screamed. "OMG," it was two in the afternoon and Yahui said that he would be here at five pm to pick me up. I had only three hours to get changed and fix my hair.

My stomach clenched and grumbled a reminder that I had yet to eat. This was gonna take some getting used to. It didn't matter that I had been eating for the last four days... never before had I needed to eat. It was a pleasure not a necessity. Now it was important to remember that I had to eat many times throughout the day. So, I only had three hours to eat, shower, change and finish getting ready.

I needed Ayi.

"Ayi?" I called out jumping out of bed and racing for the doorway. Ayi's smiling face rounded the end of the hallway carrying a tray in her arms.

"Yes, my Lady," she smiled her eyes telling me everything that her lack of words was not. "The cook has sent me up with food. It's a light lunch as you will be going out to eat before the concert."

Her mischievousness irked me. I wondered what else she was keeping in her arsenal and wasn't telling me; she sure was omniscient enough to stay one step ahead of me.

"Thank you, Ayi. You are a most treasured blessing that I could ever wish to have in a priestess, much less caretaker. I don't know what I would do without you."

"You would have found someone else worthy of your trust my Lady. It is I who you honor every day. It is truly an honor for me to bear witness to these extraordinary events." She bowed her head in respect before rising and squeezing my hand. "Xai Yahui is quite handsome my Lady. It is no wonder that your heart beats for only him. But remember-- he has only just set eyes on you five days ago. You must gain his love, not force it from him. And from all that we have learned about him. He likes to do the chasing; make him chase you my Lady. In both the real world and in that godforsaken computer game." Ayi sighed, quickly making my bed while I sat and ate my lunch.

I watched as Ayi busied herself with the fireplace. It was chilly in the room now that I wasn't bundled up in warm blankets. Finishing my brunch, I walked to the closet and found a pair of skinny black jeans without any difficulty, bending down I viewed my many pairs of footwear and I pulled out a pair of black knee high boots with a slight heel.

I remembered that Yahui had mentioned liking women who weren't too tall or too short. It brought a smile to my face wondering just how tall I am compared to him. It was hard to tell, as it had been four full days since I had stood near him and I had been wearing high heels that day. Ayi's skillful fingers shifted through the many hanging shirts and retrieved my heavy jeweled sweaters unsure of which one I would wish to wear.

I know that I had cheated in these outfit choices. I may not have seen everything in my vision, but I had most definitely seen what he was wearing for clothing. And while his sweater's jewels were vertical... mine were both horizontal. A little yang to his yin. For a moment I wondered if I should wear the silver jeggings that I bought with the black jeweled sweater, that Ayi now held aloft... I had only one way to tell. I had to try them both on and peer at my reflection in the mirror.

After showering and nearly an hour of changing back and forth, I decided on the reverse colors. Black sweater, silver jeggings and long thigh high silver boots. Ayi took to pleating a section of my hair leaving the majority of it down so that it cascaded down over the open back of my sweater.

The minute hand on the clock ticked slowly once my hair was finished. I wore only lipgloss; no other makeup was needed. After all I had natural dark long lashes and they outlined my amber eyes without need of eye liner. And while I could have added a small amount of eyeshadow I decided that none would be needed. It would only wear off if I danced and I certainly hoped that we would dance together. After watching over him all these years as he had danced, I longed to be able to feel that joy and excitement of dancing with him... On the topic of blush, well, just the thought of Yahui brought enough color to my cheeks that I could forgo the need for any artificial coloring.

That had been proven enough over the many hours of gameplay. I had thought that my cheeks would burn off from the heat he could make appear on them.

Finally, at ten minutes before the hour of five, a silver Jeep crept its way up the long driveway to my estate. The long archway of cherry trees that lined the last ten meters of the driveway bowed and waved at him as he passed by. It was only a meter more before the driveway broke off into a roundabout with a small coy pond fountain in the center island. Nia met Yahui at the door after Yahui's first knock. Welcoming him in.

Yahui wore a black pea coat opened up to the waist where he had probably just quickly buttoned it to get to the house. His hair was teased into a handsome tousled look, and the jewels on his sweater sparkled in the light of the chandelier. He walked into the center of the room where his presence automatically improved his surroundings. My eyes glanced over to him from the main hallway. I felt my legs start to tremble again at the sight of him, but they jumped at the sound of his voice. I thought that I would have grown accustomed to his tenor over these last few nights. But it was plain to see that his nearness made my body feel things that I had never once experienced in my ethereal form.

"Xai Yahui, here to pick up your Lady, ummm I'm sorry- I Still haven't acquired the Ladies name, I know her username. But I fear that wouldn't do me much good..."

"Yes Mr. Xai... My Lady will be with you shortly." Nia eyed him suspiciously... He seemed to be always on guard, Nia's eyes had never left Yahui for a second while he walked past him into the entrance foyer. I would need to talk to Nia. He need not be that weary of Yahui. I want him here. I need him to be here.

Yahui's eyes roamed over the decor and up into the post and beams that were ornately carved. Things that he failed to take in the last time he stood in this very same spot. I was very proud of my home's architecture. It felt like it was more from days long past than from the 21st century.

I couldn't put this off any longer. Taking a long, deep breath, I gathered up my courage and began my entrance into the room. At first, I kept my eyes lowered, unsure where to look. Should I stare right at him? Should I just stare at the wall behind him? I wanted to run to him, to hold him in my arms and never let him go. But I was able to keep my pace slow and my strides measured. My heart, on the other hand, raced as I looked up to find his eyes fixed onto me. A look of wonder on his face that broke into a smile that lifted higher on one side. His crooked smile. My heart leapt at the sight of it. Before I knew it, he took three long strides towards me meeting me more than halfway across the room.

"My Lady." His deep voice chimed before he bowed in greeting before me. The use of a traditional bow made me smile. I was not expecting him to use such an overlooked tradition. Rising up he leveled his tender brown eyes to mine gazing into them like he was searching for something. But before I could ask what it was, he spoke more.

"You honor me with your presence alone. That in itself would be more than enough to make this night worthwhile. But, may I be so bold as to once again ask for your name as well. It is only fair seeing as you already know my own, both online and IRL."

A lighthearted smile pulled at my lips as I thought of my best response. My smile finally won over my face making its way up to my eyes before I replied.

"Xai Yahui, if the pleasure of my company is enough to make your night worthwhile... What will my name grant you? I will allow you to call me by the name of your choosing for this evening alone. But if, by the end of this night, you want to know me more, more than a charm that you can dangle on your arm that is. I will bestow upon you my name." Yahui's eyes widened slightly and a smile crossed over his lips while I continued. "We both know that you love gaming... Think of my name as a prize that you could win. If your intentions prove true."

"Húlí, I will call you Húlí. Only for this evening, my Lady. For you have certainly outfoxed me with every step. Both IRL and in game. You have a very sharp wit. And I look forward to earning the valuable prize of your name along with your trust."

With that exchange the night began. My heart raced so hard and pounded so loudly I swore he must have heard it as he extended his arm to me. Ayi draped my own pea coat over my shoulders, a small smile playfully toyed with Yahui's lips as he noticed the color was once again in an opposite of his own pea coat. While his was black, mine was a light silvery color, with fine metallic threads holding the many black buttons into place. A true pairing of opposites, Yin and Yang: male and female.

"Húlí, I hope that you are hungry. I had the station reserve us a table at my favorite restaurant in town. They have a fantastic menu. The Hot Pot... You must have heard of it before..."

I stopped him before he could continue. "If it's your favorite I will give it a chance to impress me. I have only arrived here recently. This home was purchased only a few years ago while I was at Academy and had to be renovated before I could move in. In that regard I am a stranger to these parts. The shopping district Tuesday was my first excursion into the city." I paused letting my eyes roam over his face before adding. "And I am very fond of what I found there. So, I look forward to trying your favorite restaurant."

"Well, Húlí, you are certainly proving to be a mystery. New to the area, huh? I will have to endeavor to be your tour guide in the future."

Somehow, we had made it out to his jeep. I barely remembered moving my feet let alone walking down the short flight of stairs. He opened the passenger's side door for me and held my hand as I stepped up into his Jeep. I placed my purse down by my feet, settling in before I extended my arm up over my right shoulder reaching my hand back for the seatbelt. Only to find Yahui reaching his long arm around me.

I felt the tickle of his breath on my neck, he was so close. I could smell the intoxicating scent of his cologne. His fingers secured the belt into its latch sooner than I would have liked. Even though my face burned with heat from his nearness. I didn't want him to move away from me.

"You, sweet Húlí, are in my care. I had to swear to keep you safe." I raised my eyebrow in surprise. "Yes, Tuesday on the phone with your caretaker. She really has a way of instilling fear with a few choice words."

"Oh? Fear you say?"

"Well, yes, let's just say that I'm more afraid of what would happen to me if you were to be injured in my care." He winked, causing a feeling of fluttering to stir in my belly.

"Ahh, I see." I swallowed, attempting to keep the butterflies from flying out of my stomach. "And that was the reason you reached around me bringing your body ever closer to mine. I understand now. I may be new here, Yahui, but I do know how to buckle my own seat belt." I caught the look of guilt in his eyes before adding. "But as it is in the interest of keeping your promise, I will allow it." I tried to stifle a giggle by biting my lower lip, he bowed his head before he straightened fixing his eyes on my lips, taking full notice of my failing attempts to not laugh.

"Thank you, Húlí, I am grateful for your understanding and compliance." With utmost care he gently closed the door and ran around to the driver's side buckling his own seatbelt, before starting the engine. With his crooked smile firmly fixed to his lips, we headed off, off on what I knew would be the night that would determine my future.

More so than anyone could ever guess. More important than I even knew...For in a long-forgotten corner of the universe a long silent presence stirred. Awakening from supposed eternal slumber by the prickling of a wrong in the world. A decree somehow broken. A miss deed that he would once again have to make right. Longwei's golden eyes flashed open while thousands of miles away a lightning bolt flashed in the sky above a couple in a shiny silver Jeep.

Chapter 8

When Yahui handed his business card to the silver haired caretaker he never would have imagined that he would be faced with such an incredible female. Every aspect that he found alluring in a girl was found wrapped up in the woman who sat next to him in his Jeep.

He couldn't help but feel like he had met her before. He felt that way the moment she spoke in her estate Tuesday afternoon. But even more so since Wednesday, at Lou Hang Canyon... Like it was something from a dream, a distant memory. He stole a glance at her as he steered the vehicle down the long Main Street towards the restaurant. New Years was a big deal in the city and he had been fortunate that the station had pre reserved a table at the restaurant or they would have been hard pressed to find anywhere that had a free table before the concert.

Traffic was at a standstill, the perfect opportunity to take in this astonishing creature. Her features were so flawlessly beautiful. He kept feeling like he had met her before. Yet the where and when he had met her was eluding him. Was it just dreams? Or had he just imagined it all.

Yahui smiled as the lights from a passing car reflected and shimmered on the jewels of her sweater. When he requested that they wore matching outfits to -what did she call her- Ayi, he had only been half joking. But she went one step further making them not only match but blend a perfect balance of yin and yang. Húlí was the perfect name for her- his fox. To whom he would enjoy chasing.

The car in front of him finally started to move. Making it time to stop memorizing the way that Húlí's lips parted when she sighed. For she was sighing quite often. If he wasn't being too bold to think this but she seemed to sigh every time that their eyes would happen to meet. Even if it was just for a split second.

"The traffic is quite heavy, is it always like this?" Her sweet voice filled the interior of his jeep.

"No, actually the traffic isn't normally this heavy, but because it's the New Year's event tonight there are more people in the city. Which in turn causes there to be more traffic."

He watched as Húlí nodded in understanding. Before she spoke again. "I guess that I understand that, yet I am still amazed at the amount of traffic. Where I was before everyone walked" she paused looking over towards Yahui before she smiled slightly and continued "or rode. So, it was much less congested."

[69]

"Sounds like a very secluded place. Are you about to grant me more insight into who you are?" Yahui felt his lips curl into his crooked grin.

"No, you aren't going to trick me so easily, Xai Yahui... You won't persuade me with your Wiley ways either." She smiled that wonderful smile that met her eyes, making Yahui lose his concentration for a moment. Having to hit his brakes harder than he wanted to before swerving to miss a group of pedestrians who were camped out in the roadway. Húlí looked over at Yahui a look of concern on her face that made Yahui laugh.

"You know Ayi will keep her word." She voiced. It was meant as a retort, though moments later while she looked out the window she too began to laugh.

The restaurant finally came into view. Yahui fought back the ever-growing fear that they had missed their reservation. It was now six fifteen pm it had taken them fifteen minutes longer to get there due to the traffic. And with the line of customers that went around the back of the place they were certainly busy.

He parked the car leaving the motor running. "Húlí, please wait here while I go and check on our reservations. I will leave the motor running to keep you warm."

"Nonsense, I will go with you. If we have to wait in line, the time it takes for you to come get me will make our wait even longer." She smiled as she buttoned up her wool pea coat. Yahui shut off the ignition and shook his head as he ran around to her door. Opening it up he took her hand.

"Allow me to at least escort you properly than. Your wisdom is sound even if you are being foolish with your health."

"I will inform Ayi that if I come down sick it was my own doing and not yours."

He laughed at that shutting the Jeep's door locking it

before they started towards the restaurant's entrance. "Thank you for that offer of intervention but I fear she would demand retribution from me either way."

"True." Her Amber eyes glinted. "But I know not any other way to maintain our position in line and stay warm... Do you?"

She is baiting me. Yahui thought as he tightened his hold on her hand. Her ungloved fingers were growing cold from just this short walk.

"Your hands feel like ice..." he stopped mid stride. "Perhaps we should find someplace else to eat."

"And not eat food from your favorite restaurant? Please, don't use me as an excuse to miss out on this opportunity. I will allow you to fret over me. As long as you stop wasting time and go talk to the doorman about our reservation..."

Yahui gave a curt nod and strode towards the door.

Chapter 9

F ood is the pathway to the soule..." our waiter exclaimed, setting our dishes before us. Maybe, I thought. I'm not sure. But it sure was the way to my stomach. We had waited in line outside in the cold for thirty minutes, even though Yahui had a reservation. Before we had been seated, Yahui had placed an order, in hope that we would receive our food and finish eating before we had to leave. Ten minutes passed since we'd sat, and my body was just starting to warm up. Now that the food was here, I decided that I should remove my coat for fear that I would soil the light-colored fabric. Using chopsticks as an ethereal was one thing I could wield them with grace and finesse, along with the best of them. Eating with the fragile wooden sticks in human form wasn't nearly as elegant.

Unbuttoning the wool coat, I was instantly met with resistance. I struggled with getting it off, yet try as I might, it wasn't moving. Wool is extremely warm, but also extremely coarse when placed on top of the equally rough surface of the jeweled sweater, making the sliding off of my coat nearly impossible.

Yahui smiled as he watched me struggling, he stood up and within a heartbeat he was rounding the table. Once behind me he bent low so to whisper in my ear.

"Húlí, let me help you remove your beautiful coat. Once I take hold of the fabric around your shoulders if you stand up, I will pull your coat down over your sweater." His fingers slipped under the wool fabric pulling the wool up and over my shoulders. As requested, I stood up feeling the coat sliding off ever so slowly. Finally, I was relieved of my coat. I felt the cool breeze against the bare skin of my back the same moment that I felt Yahui's breath on my neck once again.

"Had I known that your sweater was backless I would have offered to let you sit on the opposite side of the table, with your back to the wall. I fear that you are going to draw many eyes the moment I sit back down."

"Does my sweater offend you? I never go out, so I am unaccustomed to the rules of such a thing... Please forgive my ignorance... But is it the fact that others will see my back and stare or is it that you want to be staring but cannot?"

"Húlí? You say that you are unaccustomed to dating yet you are well versed in the ways of banter. I know that from all our hours in game... Let alone the bantering that you have delivered tonight. Am I to believe that a skillful and beautiful woman such as yourself has never been out on a date?"

Smoothly I turned, taking a few steps backwards until I was in front of the opposite seat, bending I sat down in the seat that Yahui had once occupied now with my back to the wall. Yahui's eyes gleamed, had I not known better I would say that he was just as full of mischief as Ayi. He had just complimented me in the same breath as questioning my virtue. I needed to answer this as skillfully as he just commended me to be.

"Yahui," I whispered forcing him to finally sit down my Wool coat tucked into his lap. "I am neither well versed in dating nor in beauty. For I fear that I am only of average looks. There are far more beautiful than I... You, Yahui, for example, outshine me in both social and dating skills and many would probably argue that your looks outshine my own as well. For truthfully, I say to you that you are my first date."

Unwrapping the chopsticks from their napkin, I held them scissor like in my right hand picking up a steaming piece of meat. And without dropping it I brought it to my parted lips. I let my eyes gaze into Yahui's stunned ones. He watched me with a fresh set of questions dancing just beyond his reach.

"What time are we to be at the venue?" I asked once my mouth was empty "For I fear that if you only stare at me and not eat, we will surely be late."

Yahui shook his head coming out of his daydream. He stood once more placing my coat on top of his before sitting down and unwrapping the chopsticks before him. We ate in silence for several minutes. I could feel the air growing heavy between us.

My mind raced over the conversation to this point. Had I been to forward? Was he no longer interested? Such strange feelings washed over me. Lifting my eyes up slowly I chanced a glance back at his handsome face. He was beautiful. Inside and out. His brown eyes spoke more than his mouth did, yet his mouth was able to move mountains with a single sentence.

My breath caught in my throat at the way he was gazing at

me. I was reminded of another moment, another lifetime when his past-self looked at me just as he was now.

"Húlí," He breathed out finally breaking the silence. "I've sat here and watched you. Forgive me my rudeness, but I cannot help but feel that we have met before. Not like this... But in a dream that I had several weeks ago."

"Is it appropriate to talk of such things with a female that you have only recently met? Are you telling me, Yahui, that I am a dream come true?" I forced out a laugh before adding. "I fear that may sound a bit too good to be true. For I know that I have dreamed many dreams. The content of those dreams I will always cherish and hold dear. Perhaps if you prove your intentions are pure and true. I too will divulge the contents of my dreams to you."

My belly felt oddly full although I was still not finished with my meal. Lightly I dabbed my napkin to my lips before setting it down on the table. My eyes lingering on the fold of the fabric in front of me. I couldn't get up the nerve to meet his eyes again so soon after that brief exchange. I knew of the dream he spoke of. It wasn't a dream. It was reality. Twas the night before my transformation ritual. I had found him in a rehearsal room fretting about what songs to sing at this very concert. I showed myself to him, in my ethereal form all glowing and radiant.

I promised him that soon I would be standing in front of him in the flesh. For him to hold if he so dared. I had even told him that I loved him and had loved him for many centuries. Upon my hasty retreat he heard not only my words but the tolling of the bell that signaled my revelation had been detected by the powers that be. I feared that I wouldn't be able to perform the transformation because of my fool heartiness. Yet here we sat. And the songs that he was about to sing I had helped him pick out. I still pondered the reason that he had heard the bells though I was certain he had heard them because he made note of them. But I had not been able to figure that part out.

"Húlí, Please. Look at me."

His voice sounded hurt. I was confused once again. But when my eyes raised, I found Yahui not sitting across the table from me where he had been but kneeling beside me his arm resting on the back of my chair.

"I will endeavor to prove my worth to you. We must leave now, I regret to say, but I don't want to leave with you doubting that my intentions are true. If I cross a line- say something that offends you or do something that you are unsure of. Please don't hesitate to let me know. You are a rare find, Húlí, and I don't know what I have done to deserve this honor. But I will battle with anyone who tries to come between us." His eyes held mine. I thought that he was done speaking... Oh how wrong I was...

"I will court you, Húlí, like they used to in the days of old, if you will let me. I will treat you like a Princess that you are in my eyes. All these things I swear to you, Húlí... But only if you will let me."

My eyes stung and an odd feeling burned before my vision fogged. I wasn't sad. I couldn't understand the reason why I would tear up. It made no sense these human emotions. I couldn't help but wonder how they have survived for as long as they have. Yahui handed me a fresh napkin and I used it to catch the tears that were forming in my eyes.

"Thank you, Yahui. I will reflect on your offer. We have just met Tuesday after all. And you may only be saying this now.... umm... perhaps it was your drink that has allowed such words that might give a maiden hope, yet in the fresh light of day dash said hopes against the sand. Let us away. We have a concert to go to and I want to dance."

"Dance you say?" his eyes lit up once again. "I will make sure that you, Húlí, dance until your feet ache and your heart is filled with laughter." He offered me his hand and without hesitation I placed mine in his, I don't know if he felt it or if it was just me, but I felt an electric current like the ones that I had felt before when I was granting my blessings on an arranged marriage.

He interlaced his fingers with mine before he brought my hand to his lips. He kissed it softly and then pulled me to my feet. He only let my hand go long enough for us to dawn our coats and then he once again held my hand while we walked out of the restaurant, out into the cold night air where we would head off to the concert hall and hopefully a night that neither one of us would soon forget.

Lightning flashed overhead. The answering thunder shook me to my bones. It must have affected Yahui as well, for he hesitated briefly before beginning to run to the Jeep.

Húli

Chapter 10

Yahui was a different person the moment we arrived backstage at the event. Although, in all actuality he was strangely silent all the way to the venue from the restaurant as well. I understood fully that he wanted to try and save me from any added interrogation, but, I just couldn't help having this feeling that for all his good intentions he was going about this totally the wrong way. I may be wrong, of course, I smirked...this was all new territory for me, after all.

My eyes trailed after Yahui's regal form. His long strides measured and sure. His role tonight was one that he had done several times. I on the other hand, well if I was being honest this whole evening was a new experience for me. So, I matched my posture and strides to match his.

I felt an odd pulling of a smile playing at my lips while I walked through the crowded hallway. The result of a sudden thought that came to my mind... *I wonder if he is regretting his request for us to wear such noticeable wardrobe choices.* After all it was going to be blatantly obvious that we are here as a couple. The matching outfits, regardless of the fact that they were in opposite colors, were a dead giveaway.

I fought back the giggle that threatened to follow the unwelcome smile. I don't know how humans contained these impulses so well. I have so much to learn. Hopefully, I will have enough time to learn it all.

We walked a few steps a part. Only once did we lose sight of each other, granted we really hadn't *lost* each other completely and it only took me a moment to find him again. All I had to do was look for the growing swarm of females calling out his name.

Retaking my position a few steps behind and to the left him again, I followed until we arrived at a large heavy door with ornate big silver letters stenciled upon it, spelling out his name. With little apparent effort he pushed opened the door and in a graciously fluid movement he stood to one side ushering me in. I had barely walked three steps into the room, and I had heard the door shut completely, before I felt his hands gently turning me to face him.

"Húlí, are you alright? I lost sight of you for a minute and it nearly drove me insane. I was about to call out your name." He paused briefly looking me dead in the eyes. His gaze was intense and full of fear. He shook his head slightly before his lips opened again. "Granted seeing as I'm calling you a fox, which might have been a really bad idea..." He chuckled a mirthless laugh devoid of his normal jubilant tones... "I am ninety-nine percent sure that would have caused a panic." His eyes searched mine once more before he stepped back to get a better view of all of me. He looked me up and down before he dropped his hands from my arms and started pacing.

"I shouldn't have asked you to accompany me here tonight. It was selfish of me. You are going to have a lot of people scrutinizing your every move now because of me." Yahui tore off his coat and threw it at the sofa. Running both of his hands through his silky dark brown hair, causing it to spike up in places that it normally did not. The effect was quite handsome even though I knew that he didn't intend for it to be that way. He let out a sound that reminded me of an angry bear as he paced, surely he was going to wear a hole in the floor beneath him.

I unbuttoned my coat and once again struggled with the removal of it. Yahui was so preoccupied with his internal debate that he didn't notice this time. So, I had to break down and ask him for his assistance. It was either that or stay cocooned in this wooly wrapper all night. And I had no intentions of doing that.

"Yahui, umm, I'm sorry to interrupt you while your reprimanding yourself for bringing me here. But... could you take a minute and assist me in removing this horrible coat once again?"

His brown eyes softened back into his tender gaze that I had grown accustomed too. He was truly upset by something that I wasn't sure that I could fully comprehend. He strode briskly over to me. A slight twitching of a newly formed smile played at the corners of his perfect lips.

"Of course. I am so sorry for not paying attention to you, that was extremely rude of me." He bowed his head lower than before, when he straightened before he proceeded to stand behind me. "I must apologize in advance for my upcoming actions."

Confusion washed over me causing my body to stiffen. Before I could understand what he meant he pulled down the coat off of my shoulders. Once again exposing my bare skin that the backless sweater revealed. I felt a slight sensation of a feathery touch along my shoulder blades. And then the feeling of my hair cascading over my bare skin. He had just fixed my hair, yet the slight caress made my heart gallop in my chest.

"You have the most beautiful hair. At first I thought that you colored it. But now that I can inspect it closer I know that it is in fact all natural... You are all natural." He took a sharp intake of breath before he walked over to place my coat on the sofa next to where he had thrown his own. He gently laid it down smoothing the woolen fabric before his eyes turned back to me.

"Why did you agree to be my date tonight?" His voice was even but his eyes were neither warm and tender, like before, nor were they cold. But somewhere in between. I fought back my urge to tell him the whole truth- but I feared he wouldn't believe me. I needed to come up with an answer that was true so I could never be accused of lying. This must be what he had apologized for...

"Because you asked." My eyes lowered feeling shame. "I wasn't lying before when I said I have never dated. You asked, the first man to ever do so honorably. And I wanted to come."

Before I knew it, he was standing before me his hand gently raising my chin to meet his gaze. His hand may have been gentle, but his eyes had turned hard "Did you look me up? And see who I was before responding?"

"No, I neither looked you up nor did I need to. I may have lived a sheltered life, but I am not blind nor a fool. If you want to know if I knew who you were when you asked me to be your date- the answer is yes! Yes! I knew you were an actor, yes, I knew that you were a singer at tonight's event- if you must know I had already planned to attend. And yes, I know that you dance with the grace and fluidity of a breeze as it glides through the cherry trees on a summer day. I know who you are... but I knew nothing of the Yahui who can play a computer game for hours and not get tired of it... Or the Yahui who spent hours grinding levels in order to assist me in procuring an outfit for said game. Also, I did not know the Yahui who drives a Jeep through a crowded street, barely missing pedestrians because he was distracted by my presence. Neither had I known the Yahui who loves to eat at the restaurant on the far end of town. Nor did I know the Yahui who hides from the public when the spotlight is on you. Those are the Yahui's that I said yes to. Those are the man to whom I would award the prize of my true name." Tears welled up in my eyes as the heat of them burned on my flesh.

Yahui stood there in shock of my speech. We may have been out together for hours now but that is the longest that I had addressed him. Not even during our long hours of game play had I spoken to him such. My shoulders began to heave as I frantically looked around the room. Desperate to find someplace to hide. Snapping out of his shock he slowly approached. With the caution of someone who was trying to approach a wounded animal. Once he was directly before me he dropped to his knees bowing his head to the floor at my feet.

"My Lady, I am a fool. I don't even know why I doubted your integrity. It is I who asked you out after all. And I did so after seeing your beautiful face only once. If anyone should be at fault for anything it is I for being aggressive in my pursuit of you. And then to go and accuse you... I am not worthy of your name. You must think me like Dr. Jekyll and Mr. Hyde. I promise you the moon at the restaurant and the moment that I am faced with the scrutiny of the reporters I act like a raging tiger with no regard to whom I hurt in my own confusion."

My body trembled as I looked at his prone position before me. I dropped to my knees placing my hand on the back of his head.

"Please Yahui, don't feel that you have shamed yourself or me. You are weary of people who want to take advantage of you. I can understand that." I wiped my sleeve over my cheek thankful for the moment to wipe way the stray fallen tears. "Arise dear Yahui and let us start again."

Yahui sat up and looked at me. A dark line of dirt and dust went across his forehead and the tip of his nose had a covering of it as well. I couldn't help but burst out into laughter at the sight of it. I shouldn't have laughed but it was so funny, that my sides hurt from the effort of trying to stop myself from laughing.

"What?" he asked. I pointed to the corresponding areas on my own face to let him know what it was that I found so comical. He stood up with the grace of a dancer and went to the dressing room mirror. Biting his lower lip (which made my cheeks flush) he shook his head looking down at me sitting still on the floor clutching my sides. Grabbing wipe after wipe from the makeup remover canister on the counter, Yahui proceeded to scrub the offending areas. Once his face was clean, he made to dust off his pant legs before walking over to stand in front of me.

"You know this is why bowing has fallen out of everyday use in our society." he rubbed his hand over his forehead. "Did I get it all?" he asked taking my hands into his, he hoisted me up like I weighed nothing at all. Smiling I nodded, afraid that I would start laughing again if I dared to open my mouth.

"So, you thought that was funny, huh, Húlí?"

"Oh, yes..." I giggled. Unable to stop myself. "That was extremely funny. I have never seen anything like it in my life." my voice was bright, still ringing with the after-effects of the laughter. I felt a smile pulling on my cheeks. I sighed before wiping another tear, once again, from my eye.

"I love the way you smile." he whispered. Nearly too low for me to hear over the growing noise outside in the hallway. Yahui cleared his throat and then looked me over checking to see if I had any of the offending dirt on my clothing. Somehow, I had only a little on one of my boots but nothing other than that.

"Do you want to freshen up? There is a restroom through there. Once you are done, I will take you to a place that we can dance. I promised that you would dance until your feet were sore and your heart was full of laughter. I will make good on my promises, all of them."

I nodded and headed to the restroom. Yet another necessity that I needed to get used to. I had only been awake for less than a week and I think I had used the bathroom perhaps three times each day in the four full days. This would be the second time today. I would need to ask Ayi if this is normal.

Washing my hands, I stopped and looked at myself in the mirror. *Not too bad* I thought before running my fingers through my hair in the attempt to make it look exactly like how Ayi had. When my hand reached the back of my head, I couldn't help remembering the feeling of Yahui's fingers as they had lightly caressed my back. I sighed leaning into the door relishing the memory. As if on cue, Yahui called through the door startling me.

"You alright in there?"

"Yes," I responded placing my hand on the doorknob I tried to pull it open but was met with instant resistance. It took only a moment to remember that I needed to turn the knob first.

From being able to walk through walls to having to remember to flush the toilet, and turn a door knob. I certainly had a lot to learn.

Finally, opening the door, I walked out into the room only to find that Yahui wasn't alone...

"Wow... Yahui. So. She said yes after all." A short stocky man that I remembered Yahui being with several times when I would watch him in my ethereal form, stood with Yahui. I also remember seeing him running with Yahui as they fled the shopping district Tuesday. Perhaps he is a close friend of Yahui's. I felt that I should have already known his name. Yet, for the life of me, I couldn't remember his name.

"Yes, she did. Húlí, this is my friend, photographer, and manager Hou Haku... Haku let me introduce you to..."

"A fox? I think that someone miss named you, perhaps they should have called you Vixen." Haku laughed but Yahui glared at him in response. "Sorry... It is my pleasure to meet you Húlí..."

Crossing my arms over my chest I glared at Haku. "Húlí is my name for this evening only. I'm sure that Yahui will tell you all about it at some point. But I will agree with you on one count, the pleasure is all yours." I smiled at Yahui, noticing the grin that was forming on his lips from my retort. It was obvious that Haku was oblivious to the meaning of Yahui's grin, and neither one of us was about to explain.

"Haku says that there is a dance party going on in one of the backstage rehearsal rooms. The only problem is that it has a number of press members there as well. I wanted to ask you what you wanted to do before we went."

My thoughts went back to how distant Yahui was when we first entered the venue; when he ignored me and kept his distance. I needed to know if this is what I was to expect when we entered the rehearsal room. The only question that I had was a very straight to the point one. I was putting this whole night into one single response. For whatever he said will determine my own.

"Yahui, do you want to be seen with me?"

"Of course he does... You went out to eat with him didn't you?" Haku scoffed rolling his eyes before dropping down to sit on the sofa.

Never once did my eyes break from Yahui's. Though I was certainly addressing Haku. The venom in my voice was something that surprised even me. "Is your name Yahui? I thought that Yahui just introduced me to you and that your name is Haku? Am I mistaken?"

"No, you are not mistaken, Húlí. He doesn't know what you are talking about like I do. But his answer is still correct regardless... Yes, I would love to be seen with you. But it will mean your world will be different. And I will need to know your true name, now instead of later..." Yahui walked over to me, placing his hands once again on my arms. "Húlí, do you want to be seen with me?"

Leaning in toward him, I brought my lips close to his ear, whispering my response so that he alone would hear.

"My name is Wu Lihwa, and my answer is a resounding yes."

"Let's dance..."

Chapter II

When Haku said the rehearsal room had TV reporters and members of the press in attendance he meant it. Once Yahui and I walked hand-in-hand into the room all of the dancers on the dance floor stopped and every eye and camera were trained on us. I half expected Yahui to release my hand and try to distance himself like he did earlier. Except this time, he pulled me closer, moving us into the middle of the dance floor.

Lowering his mouth to my ear, Yahui spoke over the music and the new chattering of voices, with a gleam in his eyes. "You say you can dance... Think you can follow my lead?"

Pressing my index finger into the center of his chest I gave my response... "Let's find out...shall we?"

It was almost like the DJ was waiting for Yahui's signal, for with one nod from Yahui the DJ switched the music to one with a more rhythmic beat. A circle formed around us, giving us enough room to dance yet still staying close enough that I felt every eye staring at the two of us.

"Let's dance...." He caught my eyes looking at the crowd as they encircled us. "Pay them no attention," he said. "Right now, it's only you and me, okay?"

A smile lit my face at his words. It was the title of the song he would be performing in less than an hour. My heart felt like it was going to burst from the look on his face. He started to dance, slowly at first, then he began to move faster. I watched for only a moment before I mirrored his dance moves. Soon we were dancing in unison. It was like we had rehearsed for hours, instead of having never once danced with each other before. Watching over him was certainly proving to be useful in more ways than one...

Yahui's eyes glinted before he threw in a new step. I picked it up a second behind but was able to catch up, until once again we moved in sync. The crowd clapped and cheered and I was able to see the flashes of multiple cameras as I turned and swayed. But I tuned them out the best I could.

Yahui moved in closer to me when the song changed into a ballad. Wrapping his arm around my waist he pulled me to him. I leaned my head back while he spun us around, my hair fanning out behind me. I couldn't help but laugh out loud before I looked up meeting his gaze.

"We are going to be the talk of the nation in a few hours."

he called out. Smiling his perfect grin. "I have never met someone who could keep up with me like that. You my dear are a fantastic dancer." He nearly shouted this in my ear for he feared his voice would be lost over the deafening combination of music and voices. The rest of the crowd had moved in filling the void that was our dancing space just moments ago.

"Maybe you are just a great teacher." my response was met with a laugh.

"Hardly... What Academy did you attend? Was it dancing that you majored in?"

"Oh? I see, already trying to learn more about me, are you? I think that you are going to have to take me out again to get that answer. Besides, you already know my name, a prize I wasn't planning on awarding tonight... Truly I don't even know if I would have told you on our next outing ... but possibly another time if you continue to be a man of honor."

His lips formed into the cutest little pout, before he smiled once again. "Okay. Fair enough. I will reserve my personal questions until our next outing..." his smile turned into his crooked grin and with a quick movement he had me lowered into a dip. Bringing his lips down once again to my ear. His words tickled my neck with each breath... "What are you doing tomorrow?"

"Hmmm. I don't know; I might have plans to spend the day with this man I talked to Tuesday, he seems to have first seen me at a photo booth in the shopping district... He is rather handsome after all." He lifted me into a standing position, though still holding me close.

"I didn't first see you at the photo booth... I saw you the moment that you stepped foot out of the SUV. So, I guess I need to go and challenge this man to whom you speak of." He winked.

I was struck speechless. My whole body went stiff. I had been under the impression that he hadn't seen me until I was walking into the photo booth. My heart fluttered and I felt a flush of heat on my cheeks. Yahui released my waist and took hold of my hands.

"You look like you could use a drink... Can you walk? Or would you rather I carry you?"

Closing my eyes briefly I laughed. "If you are to carry me you can only do so on your back..." I had watched couples give what was called 'piggyback rides' and I so wanted to experience that with Yahui...

Before I could finish the sentence, he turned quickly, bending down before me, arms out at his sides to catch my legs once I jumped up.

"Hop on!" He shouted over his shoulder. A sly grin pressed to his lips.

I don't know what I was thinking. Perhaps the truth of the matter was that I wasn't thinking at all. Whatever the reason, whether it was because I wanted to hold him close or I was just automatically responding to his request. Either way, I gave Yahui a curt nod, took a few steps back and ran forward leaping up onto his back before wrapping my arms snuggly around his neck.

I felt his arms tighten around my thighs moments before he started walking. We maneuvered through the crowd and managed to steer clear of the majority of the reporters. Though I am sure that every last one of them had noticed the candidness of our actions.

If they had thought I was just a colleague before, now they would certainly know that we were more than that, regardless of the fact that we were still getting to know each other. Courting, Yahui had said earlier. I wondered still if he truly meant those words. I had existed too long to think that everything was settled. Too many things could still go wrong, and while he said he would court me like they did in the days of old, he hadn't said the words that would make my human existence permanent. He said that he loved my smile... But that wasn't enough. No... Not nearly enough to finalize the transformation.

Yahui stopped by a long table full of different beverage bottles, many teas, waters, and some alcoholic drinks. The music was still loud, but he didn't need to yell for me to hear him at this distance from the dance floor.

"Lihwa," He paused, a huge grin on his face. "Sorry, I just realized that is the first time I've actually said your name. Lihwa." He released one of my thighs and I lowered my foot to the floor before he released the other. Taking my hand moments before it slipped completely off his shoulder, he turned to face me. "Correct me if I'm wrong... But doesn't your name mean 'Princess?'"

"Yes, you are correct," he said, nodding slowly, his thumb making little circles on the back of my hand. He neither moved nor spoke, and I felt a wave of uncertainty crash over me. My next words flowed from my lips before I could even think them through. "Do you not like my name?"

His eyes shot up to mine. The intensity of his gaze made me inhale sharply. "Yes, Lihwa, I really do like your name. Don't ever let anyone tell you that your name is ill fitting. When they named you, they certainly choose wisely."

"Thank you, Yahui." I closed my eyes and started to bow my head only to have Yahui's hand once again on my chin forcing me to meet his eyes. "You have nothing to thank me for. I only spoke the truth. Your name is as lovely as you. I fear that you misread my silence and for that I am sorry. I was merely thinking... We are here surrounded by prying eyes and shameless snoops, after all. Lihwa, I need to do an interview shortly, and they are going to ask me about you. I want to know if you would be alright if I said we are courting... Or would you be more comfortable with telling them that we are dating? I don't want to tell them something that you aren't comfortable with them running."

"Running? Ah, printing or airing. Sorry, my mind is just racing. Yahui, you can tell them that we are seeing each other exclusively. Would that satisfy their desires?"

"Exclusively, huh?" Yahui reached out and fingered a strand of hair that had managed to work its way loose when we were dancing. Tucking it tenderly behind my ear he let his hand linger on the side of my face. Leaning in closer to my ear he whispered. "I like the sounds of that." His breath on the side of my neck sent a pleasant shiver down my spine. He stepped back grabbing two bottles of tea. "Here... This is my favorite flavor of tea." He handed me the bottle. The coldness of the container felt incredible against the increasing heat in my hand. "I hope that you like it."

"I'm sure I will." I watched him twist the cap off with a swift motion of his wrist and I copied his movements to open my own. Bringing the rim of the bottle to my lips I let the cold liquid pour into my mouth. The tea was sweet with a hint of mint. I smiled at the flavor, remembering my water that has become my favorite drink while at the estate. "Mmm, it is really good. I love the mint. I enjoy mint in my drinking water."

Yahui smiled, "I do too. Not many of my friends do though so it is nice to know that we have that in common as well."

"Oh? What are the other things we have in common?" I asked before bringing the bottle to my lips for another sip.

"Oh, from what I have seen tonight we have a few things in

common. Not to mention all the hours we spent gaming over the last few nights ... So, let me see..." He pauses bringing his free hand to his lips tapping his index finger to his top lip repeatedly while he leaned back against the wall besides the table. "Hmm, let's see, although you aren't a true gamer... I think I can say that we share a common interest in the freedom that that world allows. Also, we both have a passion for dancing. I would say that you probably have some training. You like Hot Spots like I do, and we share a similar taste in fashion. Add on to that the fact that we like the same tea." He brought the tea bottle up shaking it before continuing. "And we both take our drinking water with mint in it, I would say that we have quite a few known things in common. I believe that we might find more commonalities in the days to come." dropping his voice down low he continued .. "I for one am looking forward to discovering those commonalities along with the hidden things that might be our differences as well."

I had to restrain myself from outright laughing. The one major difference between us, might be the one thing that will make or break us. I can only hope that it will be the former. For I know I wouldn't survive the latter. *Literally.* Instead I smiled as demurely as I could before responding to his admission.

"Yahui, I look forward to getting to know you better as well."

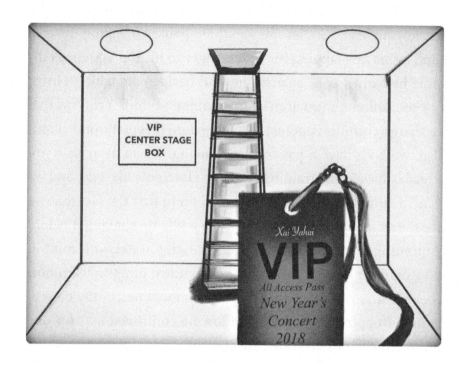

Chapter 12

It was ten thirty-five when we left the rehearsal room depositing our empty bottles into the recycling bin. We exited through the door and headed down the hallway. It was time for him to do his interview and I would need to find the seat that was reserved for Yahui's 'plus one' as Haku called it. Apparently it was close to the stage where he would be performing, and I was anxious to be able to witness his show as a human. I had seen him perform before, of course, yet I was determined to continue counting the firsts in this new body.

Stopping outside of a large set of double glass doors Yahui grabbed my hand pulling me into a warm hug. It was an amazing feeling. My body quivered briefly before relaxing in his arms. I don't know how long our embrace lasted but even if it had lasted until the end of time before releasing, our parting would have come too soon.

"Go sit. I will find you in the audience... I think that you should have a decent vantage point. At least I was told you would have a good one. Close to the stage..." He paused squeezing me tighter... "If I need another dancer, I might have to pull you onto the stage to back me up." he laughed as he reluctantly pulled away. He looked into the room at the growing crowd of reporters who waited for him. "Wish me luck, they look like they are circling sharks. Waiting for the next juicy piece of gossip to chew on."

"You sure you don't want me to go in with you?" I asked meaning every word. I would face the hungry sharks and gladly feed them the information that they would be hunting me down for in the coming weeks.

"Not this time. But I fear that we may need to face them together soon enough. Thank you for your sweet bravery. Go. Enjoy the show. I will deal with these sharks tonight." He rubbed my arms quickly up and down warming me with the friction.

"Good luck, Yahui." I said with a nod lifting my hand two fingers up. I gave him a peace sign with a smile and a tilt of my head. He chuckled and patted his hand lightly on the top of my hair carefully so not to mess it up.

"Go on now, before I do drag you in there with me... Or I ruffle up your hair. Whichever comes first."

Walking away from him felt like someone was tearing a part of me off slowly and painfully. I had to keep reminding myself that I would see him soon. Haku was waiting at the end of the hallway to lead me down along darkened passageway that ended at a set of doors that opened upwards. I needed to climb up a short ladder in order to go through them to a small box seating section. There were only four seats in this particular box, and we were the only ones in it. Haku shut the doors behind himself while I took the seat closest to the stage. I must admit if Yahui reached out his hand from the stage we might truly be able to touch.

Currently the stage was occupied by a group of four announcers all formally dressed. The two men wore suits and the two ladies wore beautiful red dresses. I had obviously missed a portion of their dialogue, but it was evident that they were talking about the upcoming performers that I could see the stagehands diligently preparing for.

"Yahui is due to perform after the next act completes their set. I must admit, I would have never thought that Yahui would be a taken man at the ringing in of the new year. Especially not when I had to drag him to the shopping district Tuesday morning. His original plus one fell sick and cancelled on him, you see. So, I wanted to help him find a replacement." He beamed as he looked over at me pulling a thread from his frayed jean coat's sleeve. "I guess you could say I am responsible for you two meeting."

"I guess, perhaps I should thank you then." I answered before looking back out over the stage... "Haku?"

His face lit up. "Yes?"

"Who was the girl who took ill?"

Crestfallen Haku sighed then slouched back in his seat before answering. "One of his costars... His fans had voted for him to either have her as his date or for him to bring a fan as his plus one. Many of his fans have shipped Yahui and Lui Wei. SO... they were hoping that they would start seeing each other as a couple not as just friends."

"I see... You think that Yahui's revelation that we are

exclusive will be met harshly?" even as I asked this question, I knew the answer.

"Lihwa, there is no easy way to say this. So, I will just come out and tell you like it is." Haku shifted in his seat leaning forward to meet my gaze. My eyes searched his hoping that he was going to tell me something I already didn't know. "You are going to find that some of Yahui's fans will love the idea that he has finally found someone. While the other part, the ones who voted for him to bring Lui Wei here tonight for example, they will be the ones who will put up the most resistance and make the most commotion. Sadly, that is the truth of the matter."

"Thank you, Haku, for your honesty. I know that there's going to be a lot of naysayers, and we will probably have a ton of hate mail for a while. But I hope that I can win the majority of them over in time." The lights flashed several times over head and the announcers introduced an act that I was unfamiliar with. Yet Haku seemed to recognize them. Calling out along with the crowd shouting out a few hoot and holler before attempting to sing, albeit out of tune, along with the song.

I let my mind wander over all of the events of this evening so far. Recalling all of the finer points and scrutinizing the not so great parts. I needed to make sure that I wasn't acting as the pursuer. No matter how much I would like to divulge everything to Yahui. I needed to let him set the pace. I felt that I certainly had been doing just that. I even let him talk me into playing a MMORPG computer game into the wee hours of the morning after all... I paused in that thought... *Ok so I really have enjoyed playing the game with Yahui the last four nights.* But it was his idea to start with and if that wasn't allowing him to set the pace, I don't know what is.

The band on stage surprisingly only performed one song. While it was certainly long, it finished before I knew it to the loud applause of the crowd. One of the male announcers called out over the cheers of the crowd, stating that there would be a short break as the stage was readied for the next performer... When he hollered Yahui's name the crowd screamed in appreciation, and I found myself joining in. It may have only been a handful of minutes since we had parted, yet, I was already more than eager to see him again.

Chapter 13

Walking into the shark pit was daunting at the best of times, and that was when Yahui was only having to think of his own personal welfare and privacy. Walking into the center of the swarming sharks with the well-being of another's life was quite a different story.

Taking a deep breath Yahui opened the double glass doors. Making an entrance was a good way to show his resolve, and the gods knew he needed all of the resolve he could muster.

When Lihwa offered to join him in this pit. He was honestly moved beyond words. He had dated before in the past. In all actuality he had dated more than his fair share of women (most of them also being celebrities), but all of those relationships had been kept as secret as possible. Several times, in fact if a rumor of their dating started to circulate, both parties adamantly denied the existence of such a relationship. Claiming to only be friends because of the fear of what such a relationship could do to both their careers and their personal lives. This time he felt differently about the public knowing. This time he didn't want to have to date in secret. This time he wanted the world to know that she was his.

All eyes followed him while he strode up to the small makeshift stage. A single chair was facing the crowd with several microphones lined up in front of it.

Quite a few of the reporters were familiar to Yahui, interviews after all were old hat to him now. Having been in the spotlight for just over seven years. But there were a handful of reporters here that he had never seen before. One such reporter seemed very keen on staring at him. His eyes were harsh and yet that wasn't the only thing imposing about him.

He was a mountain of a man; his pure mass made the rather large chair he sat on seem tiny in comparison. Yet, Yahui had known his fair share of gentle giants in his life so he didn't want to pass judgment without just cause. In all actuality he wouldn't have given the man any extra attention had it not been for the way the man was staring at him.

This man's unwavering scrutiny made Yahui feel... *defensive*, somehow... That was the only way to explain it.

Shaking these feelings off as jitters, he did his best to make himself comfortable in the "Hot Seat". With a well-rehearsed smile placed on his lips, Yahui cleared his throat and greeted the hungry predators.

"Good evening everyone! I want to thank you for having

me here tonight. I'm sure that you're all aware that I will be ushered out of here in about twenty minutes. Let us begin."

All at once hands raised into the air. Yahui nodded at one reporter who he remembered seeing in the rehearsal room just moments ago. Yahui was almost certain that he knew what this reporter would ask. Better to get this question over with first thing. Then they would take the long road down the landslide of questions that this one would create.

"Xai Yahui, thank you for acknowledging me first. Your kindness has always known no bounds. It has come to our attention this evening that you are in the company of a mysterious female. When we heard the report that Lui Wei had canceled on you for this evening due to sickness. I must admit that I didn't expect to see you here with anyone other than your normal entourage. Seeing the young lady by your side upon arrival made us all take notice. Are you and her seeing each other? Or are you just really close friends or possible family? Let me rephrase that... Just who is she?"

"Thank you for your kind words. It was a shame that Lui Wei could not be here tonight. She and I are really good friends and I hope she feels better soon.

As for my date this evening," Yahui paused looking out at all the eager faces. Picturing Lihwa's sweet face he drew in a deep breath and smiled wistfully. "She is very dear to me. Her name is Wu Lihwa and we are exclusively seeing each other."

The clamoring of the crowd was exactly what he expected with this admission. Several voices called out his name while some reporters stood up to gain Yahui's notice, hopeful that this action would get them called upon first. With one hand resting on his lap while the other was cupping his chin Yahui smiled, the trueness of his smile shown in his eyes, and he sighed before calling on yet another reporter. This time one of the unfamiliar ones.

"Xai Yahui, when will we get to meet Wu Lihwa? When you say exclusive, I get the feeling that this relationship has been going on for some time. Forgive my bluntness, but this is the first time that you both have been seen in public together."

"No it isn't. We have been seen together in public besides here. It's just that there were no reporters there to take notice. Forgive me for saying this but thankfully reporters such as yourselves aren't always in every public space." It wasn't a lie after all. They didn't need to know that the time he was talking about was just earlier that very same night.

The mountain of a man in the back stood up and before being called on he asked his question in a booming voice.

"Would you say that your relationship with Wu Lihwa is serious?"

Normally Yahui wouldn't have answered a question from a person who displayed such a blatant disregard for the rules of the *pit*. But he felt compelled to respond to this immense presence. Yahui felt like he had just been challenged by the schoolyard bully. Lowering his hand from his chin he leaned forward squaring his shoulders in the process. "Sir, I think the fact that we are exclusively seeing only each other answers that question. But maybe I was vague in my description. Lihwa is extremely dear to me. I would battle anyone who intended to try and take her. Furthermore, I am hopeful that our relationship will continue to grow into one that will be remembered, cherished, and looked at as an example of how love is supposed to be for several generations to come! So yes Sir, I believe that our relationship is very serious."

Yahui could have heard a pin drop there was such a quiet hush. Yahui had never before let an interviewer affects him so. Every muscle in his back and arms where taunt. Even the hand he had relaxed in his lap was clenched into a tight fist. Forcing his trademark grin onto his face, Yahui relaxed his hand just a moment before a young webinar reporter tentatively raised her own.

Yahui smiled and acknowledged her, thankful for her bravery... He was worried for a minute that he had totally ruined the course of the interview. She rose to her feet with a look of awe in her eyes.

"Yahui ... umm Sorry, Xai Yahui. Thank you for your candor. I have never once heard of a star of your caliber being so forthright in discussing their romantic lives before. And for that I want to sincerely thank you." she looked down at the floor quickly before continuing on with her question. "We would, I mean I think I speak for everyone here when I ask this, but we would all love to know what in particular attracted you to Miss Wu?"

Leaning back fully into his seat Yahui laughed slightly rubbing his index finger in the curve between his bottom lip and his chin. "That is an interesting question. Let me think." Yahui gazed down at his lap a small area of dirt caught his attention, and he let his fingers run over the area as his smile grew into one of pure wonder and joy. Nodding, he sighed, looking at the young reporter before him.

"For those of you who have already seen Wu Lihwa, you all know and can attest to the extent of her natural beauty. But what you didn't and couldn't possibly see, because you couldn't tell with just a glance, is her amazing spirit and the beauty that lies within. She is truly a fascinating woman. Who engages me both logically, with her intelligence and wit, and physically."

Yahui looked out over the audience looking for the faces he had noticed in the rehearsal room. "Earlier, as some of you saw, we had a dance challenge, and without rehearsal she was able to mirror my impromptu dance moves. Better than any of the dancers that I have been dancing with for years could ever do. It was incredible to see from my standpoint... I can only imagine what everyone else thought." A number of the reporters who were in the rehearsal room and had witnessed their dancing, all nodded in agreement. "Other than those important factors, Wu Lihwa is just a very unique soule. She actually volunteered to attend this interview with me, to come out to all of you. I told her I wanted to address you all by myself this time. Although, I will be happy to ask her to do an interview with me in the near future." a waving arm by the backstage door caught Yahui's attention. Twenty minutes had sure flown by quickly. Yahui stood and addressed the crowd. "I need to get ready to perform. To everyone who I was unable to answer your questions this evening, please forgive me. Twenty minutes isn't enough time to get to all your burning thoughts. I ask that you write down your most important ones in a list (please keep it to no more than two each) and give them to my publicist. I will attempt to respond to them all, within reason of course, over the next coming weeks. Thank you for your time"

Yahui raised his hands palms together in front of him, genuflecting. Rising after a few moments, Yahui took a few steps off the platform towards the doorway at the back of the room that would bring him directly to the stage.

Yahui felt the eyes of the rude reporter burning into him with their intensity. Staring straight ahead Yahui took the measure of the man from the corner of his eye. The man was fierce looking to say the least. He sported a full growth of facial hair that looked as though it had never seen the use of a comb.

His storm filled golden eyes made Yahui feel extremely on edge. Wanting to get a better look at the man Yahui chanced a brief peek back over his shoulder once he got to the door and while the glimpse was for only a second, the look on the man's face was enough to make Yahui want to wrap Lihwa up in his arms and protect her, running away to the ends of the earth if possible.

The mountain of a reporter was still staring at Yahui, but now he had a glint in his eye that Yahui could only describe as one of pure malice. With a newfound determination, Yahui pushed open the stage door and swore to himself that he would do everything in his power to make his response to that man a reality. Not just some pretty, well-rehearsed, words that you say in an interview and not mean, he would fight to secure a future with Lihwa.

The stage manager handed Yahui his headset microphone and the battery pack/transmitter. He hooked the transmitter to the waistband of Yahui's jeans before threading the wires for the microphone and the earpiece up the inside of the back of his sweater keeping them out of sight. The cool wires rubbed over the bare skin of his back, a feeling that he had gotten used to over the years.

Looking out over the crowd from this vantage point, he was able to immediately pick out Lihwa in a viewing box next to the stage. She was sitting so primly in her seat. The picture of a perfect young lady. A 'Princess' to the letter. Her jeweled sweater glistened with each pass of the stage's strobe lights.

Normally he would be fighting back a mild case of stage fright at this point. He had always feared that he wasn't as good a singer as he was a dancer. But for some unknown reason tonight's performance was different. Everything about tonight had been different than he had ever experienced before. The only reasonable conclusion was that it was all because of this incredible woman that had come into his life. Making it into something that was worth fighting for. Not that he had ever been the type who would ever give up and quit, but now there was a driving force that was bigger than before, when he was fighting for only himself.

He smiled broadly when the announcers called his name. A mirror image of the smile he saw Lihwa wear as her ever attentive eyes search the stage. Her smile warmed his heart making him smile twice as big as he was before.

The lights went out and the stage manager spoke into Yahui's earpiece.

"Time to get into position, Xai Yahui."

Chapter 14

Even before the first notes of music started, I could make out Yahui's distinct outline on the stage. It didn't matter that he had a group of dancers around him I could identify him in a crowded room if need be. Even in my human form I could make out the distinct aura that was unmistakably that of my soule mate.

Most of the lights were already out above the stage, and the crowd for that matter, but all the other lights flickered. I knew that this wasn't the normal flickering, because even the emergency exit sign's lights had fluttered in and out. It was for the briefest of moments really, just a second but the seriousness of it could be tragic. I heard a man behind me snicker. I didn't know who it was, but I didn't find it at all funny. It would be horrible if the power went out, especially just before Yahui was to perform.

My nerves felt like I was on high alert when a moment later a small waft of fog began to gather at the edges of the stage. Slowly at first, curling over the edges playfully rolling out into the crowd, before the fog started to thicken. Becoming more like a dense cloud of smoke that totally enveloped Yahui and his dancers. Hiding them completely from view. It was a hauntingly familiar memory, a smoke screen. My heart began to race, I felt it pounding out a drumline in my chest.

A number of years ago Ayi had requested that I phase to a country on the other side of our massive continent, a request that I was confused by, at first. After all, why would I want to travel to a land that was so unlike my own. But the trip proved invaluable. That is why I chose one of the French Academies to be my Alma mater. I attended classes there, not only in a corporeal form. I learned all about art, how to draw and paint, I took dancing lessons and I even became involved in theater as well. I learned many foreign languages, I can speak a total of seven fluently from English all the way to, of course, French. At this very moment I had a very strong feeling of what the French would call Déjà vu, and it was tying my stomach up in knots, regardless of what I called it the sight of my love surrounded by smoke set my body into a sense of panic.

"Haku? Where is that smoke coming from? Is the stage on fire?" my voice quaked while my body trembled. Desperate to get answers I grabbed on to Haku's arm, shaking it hard I repeated my questions this time I was nearly screaming each one in his ear.

His eyes grew large in surprise before I could see a dawning understanding there.

"No need to worry, Lihwa. It's just smoke from a fog machine. It's special effects. Nothing is the matter and no need for alarm. You can relax, I promise." He looked down at my fingers that were digging into his tattooed flesh of his forearm. "Can I have my arm back?"

"Sorry."

At his words I willed my body to release his arm, I tried to do just that, relax. But much like before it was easier said than done. When I was at the estate I had held my knees to my chest, that might have helped than but doing that here would certainly draw unwanted attention and I didn't want to worry Yahui when he happened to look this way. I forced myself to smile...

The electronic tones of the synthesizer flooded my ears and the lights came up revealing Yahui and his dancers safe and sound on the stage for all to see... Relief poured over me, like I had just taken a refreshing dip into a lukewarm bath. I felt the panic totally disappear from my body. His eyes caught mine and with a quick wink he began his performance.

Before my transformation I had watched Yahui perform, probably more times than even Ayi knows about. I couldn't even begin to count the way that this was different. Perhaps it was the millions of nerve endings that this human body afforded me, or perhaps it was the fact that this time, for the first time, Yahui knew that I was there. He would periodically look my way and my heart would race. I felt it pounding in my chest. For these reasons alone this was the best performance by him that I had ever witnessed. Each beat of my heart sang out three words over and over: I love him. I love him.... I have always loved him.

Yet, I must admit, for some unknown reason there was an added sensation with this reincarnation. I felt it from him even when I was still in my ethereal form. I just couldn't put my finger on what it was, and honestly as long as we are together, for as long as we both shall live. I found myself not caring. If at some point it becomes something that I need to worry about. I will deal with it then, but right now. I thought gazing at him dancing just an arm's length away from me, I will refuse to look for trouble where there wasn't any to find. Each second with him was too precious to waste on such trivial issues. Even if the time spent was battling monsters online together.

The last chorus of his song floated from his hypnotic lips finding me waving my hands in the air like so many of the other concert goers around me. Yahui's eyes locked on to me. His shoulders rising and falling with each rapid breath, he was breathing harder than he had when we danced in the rehearsal room. Still he looked so incredibly handsome that it should be criminal. From the sly look on his face I believed that he knew I couldn't tear my eyes from him. Nor did I want to.

It wasn't until he placed his fingers to his lips that he totally rendered my heart to a melted mush. Because in one fluid motion he blew me a kiss. Haku chuckled at the obvious show of affection on Yahui's part.

"He is gonna hear it tomorrow on all of the social media sites. Every female fan in this direction is gonna post that he was flirting with them." He scoffed shaking his head. "They have probably already started posting it, with video proof." His eyes glanced over to me for a moment before with a deep sigh he added. "He even has you blushing so much that your cheeks are the perfect match for our announcer's dresses."

My hands flew to my cheeks as I smiled uncontrollably. I knew he was right... If I had one hundred yuan for every fan who thought that kiss was for them. I could easily become a millionaire ten times over. Placing my right hand over my lips I blew him a kiss back. Yahui smiled broadly reaching up his hand acting like he snatched my kiss from the air and the next moment he gave a finger heart to the audience to cover his response before walking over to the beckoning announcers.

One of the female announcers addressed him. "Xai Yahui, Let's hear it for Xai Yahui…. That was a fantastic performance. I hear that you have a second song for us this evening."

"Thank you, Thank you so much for your kind words. Yes, I do have a second song that I will be singing here in a few moments."

"Excellent. That is great to hear. A number of tonight's performers have only done one song before finishing up their set. With the new year growing closer. It's one hour away folks, it will be wonderful to have your music to help us usher it in." The crowd cheered and the announcer waved her arm… Smiling she turned her attention back to Yahui… "Xai Yahui. Do you have any special New Year's wishes or plans?"

"Actually, I do. I have someone who I plan on spending my free time with this coming new year. As you all know I have a full production schedule ahead of me with multiple TV dramas in the works. But if I am lucky, I will be able to talk her into doing some traveling with me."

"We heard that you have a special someone here with you this evening. Is that correct?"

My heart skipped a beat and I held my breath. I knew that in all honesty it would be easier on him tonight if he just played it off. But my heart said a silent prayer that he would actually choose to confirm this question.

Yahui looked pointedly at me. His eyes twinkled and he tilted his head to the side a silent request for my approval. I nodded and smiled, holding my hand over my galloping heart.

"Yes, she is here." There was an exciting burst of voices. Yahui looked out into the audience, addressing his many fans directly. "Would you all like to meet her?"

A deafening cry of yes from the crowd gave him the response he was looking for. As for me... My response was: WHAT? I'm pretty sure that I managed to not physically scream that out but I'm sure that my anxiety level rose. Which was yet another first that I could number, my first anxiety attack. Wishing that I had brought my purse in instead of leaving it locked up in Yahui's Jeep. I know that I looked presentable when I left for the evening but that was six hours ago.

Haku gently grabbed my arm, bringing me back to myself and to my feet. In my surprise, I had somehow *spaced* out (one of Ayi's favorite terms) for I didn't notice that Yahui had walked over to stand right in front of me. Yahui smiled and shook his head.

"You'll have to ask her nicely. I think that she is playing shy."

The crowd called out in near perfect sync, " Please don't be shy. We want to meet you."

"See that was a respectful request."

I sighed then took Haku's hand allowing him to help me stand up onto the seat. Placing one foot onto the railing, I looked into Yahui's eyes.

"Your hands please, Miss Wu." Yahui's voice echoed through the arena. I reached out taking his hands in mine and with the grace of a ballerina, I leapt onto the stage and into Yahui's awaiting arms. The crowd roared in response. Interlacing his fingers with mine he led me over to the announcers.

"Aww.... Look everyone she is wearing a matching outfit... can you all see that? A perfect yin and yang of colors." One of the male announcers stated when we came upon them.

I felt my cheeks burning crimson. Though through it all I managed to stay in step with Yahui carrying myself with the poise and grace that I knew would be expected of me.

Once we reached the main stage Yahui drew me to his side while one of the announcers handed me a microphone.

"Welcome Miss Wu.... "

"Miss Wu Lihwa." Yahui corrected.

"Miss Wu Lihwa...What a beautiful name for such a vision of loveliness. Are you having a good time this evening?"

I smiled and brought the microphone to my lips carefully angling it, I made my first public address.

"Yes, thank you, I am enjoying the performances that I have seen here this evening. I couldn't be more honored to be here sharing my New Year's countdown with all of you amazing people. Not to mention this talented performer and incredibly fantastic man, Xai Yahui." I lifted out joined hands into the air. Receiving a favorable response from the crowd I continued. "I have truly been blessed."

Yahui smiled at me a light tinging of his cheeks let me know that he was happy to have me here with him as well.

"Now that you are on the stage with Yahui are you going to join him for this last number?"

"Only if he wants me to." I answered. Looking over towards Yahui. He nodded repeatedly just like a euphoric little child with a joyful smile on his face. "I guess that means that I will be joining him."

The crowd cheered calling out my name. It was such an odd feeling. Yahui squeezed my hand then tugging it gently he maneuvered me to the side of the stage.

His hand went to his microphone covering the little mouthpiece before addressing me.

"Thank you, Lihwa. So, here is your chance to show the world your dance moves. Think you're ready?" A sly grin worked at the corners of his mouth. Stopping myself before I gave in to my sudden urge to kiss him. I forced myself to look anywhere but at his lips. Finally, giving up on the avoidance tactics I looked him dead in the eyes.

"I am no stranger to performing before an audience. Yahui. Though I would have liked to have had time to rehearse before doing this. Just lead and I will follow."

§

In all of my years of existence, I had been called on many times to perform before the greater gods. As a lesser goddess it was my duty to do as they commanded. Dancing was only one such task that I was commanded to do. And it was one of the tasks that I truly loved.

Many times, more times than I can count, I danced before them all weaving my magic through the air as I did so. Tonight's performance was not quite up to that level of expectations, but it sure felt close to it.

Once on stage Yahui began giving new instructions to his crew. Unlike the normal configuration that they would employ, Yahui had me stand two steps in front of him and just slightly off to his left. This would make it nearly impossible for me to actually follow his lead. Somehow (and by somehow, I mean I could tell by the devilish grin that he held on his lips), I felt that he purposely positioned me here so that I would have to improvise.

He wasn't totally devious; he did instruct me to hold still. He even took great pains to pose me in a position even going as far to informed me that I would hold this pose until he walked over and finished *touching* me "bringing my character into action". An action that he would conclude by grabbing one of my hands. So I did just that, I held perfectly still.

My eyes were closed with my head tilted ever so slightly

to the left. My arms were crossed over my chest with my hands resting on my shoulders. Really a comfortable position, if I had to hold it for any real length of time. My feet where even in a natural position if only slightly staggered. All in all, I couldn't complain. I had certainly been in worse poses before and had to hold them for many days, instead of just mere minutes.

The music started and I had to force myself not to smile or move. He had changed up the song list. I knew he did because this is not the second song that I had helped him pick out. Although in this situation this new selection was absolutely perfect. From the reaction of the crowd I wasn't the only one who felt that way. Falling in Love with the Madness of Loving You. The songs title said volumes, but it was one of my favorite songs by him.

Much like how someone without hearing and sight could tell that there was someone walking around them I could feel the movement on the stage of the other dancers and Yahui. I was at least aware of their general locations. It wasn't until he started singing the fifth stanza (the fifth line in the song) that I could feel the energy sparking between us because Yahui was standing directly in front of me.

My body hummed with anticipation of his touch. Yet I wasn't prepared. No, I wasn't prepared at all for his hand to move across my left cheek up into my hair, nor was I prepared for the feeling of his breath so close to my lips that if I just leaned forward a millimeter our lips would have been touching.

He didn't kiss me.

Even though I would have let him, gladly in fact. But the two of us where the only ones in the stadium who knew that for sure. He sang the next stanza still caressing my face with his hand before he took my right hand from my shoulder into his own and twirled me away from him. Once he let go and moved away I began to dance following the lead of his dance moves.

He never strayed too far from me. Several times he actually danced behind me forcing me to either turn or make up my own moves instead. It was on one of the latter choices that the crowd responded with a male dominated cheer, even Haku seemed amused by something. I was certain that it wasn't anything of my doing as the moves I was doing was ones that Yahui himself had done previously in the number.

It wasn't until the last chorus that I found out what had caused such a reaction. My actions probably had just messed up his Choreography but the moment he went behind me I turned to face him. He had an appreciative look on his face as he looked me over and before I could turn back around he slid up to me placing an arm around me with his hand coming to rest on the bare skin of my back. To say that the feeling of it was pleasant would be an understatement.

Borrowing a dance move from an old movie from the 1980s, Yahui seized my thigh in his hand pulling it up to his waist and silently directed me to arch my back into his supporting and oh so incredibly warm hand. Without a second's hesitation I complied. When I arched back, he supported me swinging my body into a semicircle before I straightened placing my forearm onto his shoulder.

There was a fire burning in his deep brown eyes while he sang about the madness of love and how he didn't care what happened in the past, he just wanted to love me crazily! The fire burned in me as well, just not exclusively in my eyes.

The last lift he performed happened so effortlessly that even I wasn't sure how or what we had just done. All I knew was that once the song finished, he had our bodies aligned in such a way that renowned Olympic pairs skaters would envy us.

Yahui's shoulders raised and fell rapidly with the effort of his exertions. The crowd went wild as did the announcers. Instead of beckoning us to them they came running over to us. But the original four were not alone. There were four other men wearing red suit jackets rushing to greet us as well.

Yahui lowered me into his arms pulling me into an incredibly tight hug and I squeezed him twice as tight in response. We were both filled with excitement. Which seemed to only be growing as he twirled us around, causing my feet to once again leave the stage...

"Be prepared. Looks like the executive producers have taken notice of you," Yahui breathed into my ear.

"Me?" I gasped looking around at the newcomers.

"Bravo, bravo!" The announcers shouted moving to stand on either side of us. Yahui set me back on the stage leaving an arm curved protectively around my waist. I found that I was more than slightly out of breath. New experience number seventeen (or was it eighteen) in this form. I struggled to catch my breath before one of the announcers asked me a question that I wouldn't be able to answer without panting like an overworked little puppy.

I wish I could sit here and say that my lack of breath was all from the exertion of dancing. But I would be a liar. That annoyance that I had experienced earlier at the estate had now taken on another form, and this feeling was something that in all my years of existence I had never once experienced.

I was quivering like the wings of a hummingbird.

Yet this time while my body was trembling so much it vibrated, mine was not the only one doing so.

Chapter 15

I was floating on a pillow top raft going down a gentle stream, swaying back and forth by pull of the current. I heard the rhythmic flow of the water all around me. Yet I did not feel its fine mist. Nor did I feel the cold winter air that I knew I should be feeling. No, instead, I felt a pleasant warmth pressing into me from my left side.

A faint yet familiar scent of men's cologne filled my nostrils. It was the pleasant scent of my love: Yahui. A low sigh passed over my lips as I nuzzled my cheek deeper into the soft warmth of my pillow. Inhaling the aroma greedily.

"Xai Yahui," I cooed with a smile dancing on my lips.

"I could listen to you say my name like that all night,

but I fear that Ayi would not approve." Yahui's musical voice surrounded me and my warm raft shook with his gentle laughter. It was then that my eyes flashed open with a start.

"Yahui? Oh no. No, no, no. Please forgive me. Our date? I fell asleep. I'm sorry." My voice was frazzled, each word stumbling over the next. I gently pushed myself away from his chest in an effort to gain my bearings, besides being in his arms I had no idea where we were, and being this close to him was certainly making it hard to even think straight.

"Hold still now or I'll end up dropping you. We are nearly to your estates front door." Yahui pulled me back to his chest, I gave in without complaint. "Allow me to deliver you safely home. You have had an exciting couple of hours. Lots to mull over."

Placing my head back onto his shoulder I let out a long wistful sigh. He wasn't totally wrong, nor was he fully correct in that statement. I have experienced the most exciting night of my life, not just the last few hours of it.

I had gone out to eat (with Yahui), had a dance off in a rehearsal room (with Yahui), been outed as Yahui's exclusive girlfriend not only to the press, but to the world (At least everyone who was watching the live broadcast). Danced on stage in front of thousands of cheering fans (again with Yahui), not to mention that we had everyone thinking that we actually kissed on stage, and finally, was offered a role in one of the upcoming tv dramas that Yahui would start filming in the next few months. They wanted us to come and do a test scene together. We would hear more about when in the next few days.

With everything that happened from five until midnight I would say that I had a fantastic night until somehow or another I managed to fall asleep, and had woken up in the arms of the man that I love (not saying that part wasn't a good thing mind you), the man that I had taken human form for. It had been a night to remember, I knew that I would never forget it.

Yahui's shoulders shook gently. Obviously laughing at my reaction or the lack of my normal banter, more likely. With his arms cradling me, he walked up the stairs and had barely stepped foot on the doorstep when the door flew open, revealing the concerned face of my dear Ayi.

"Oh god, is she alright?" Ayi's lower lip trembled as she flipped on the outside light blinding me with its sudden brightness.

"I was until you took away my sight." I laughed attempting to shield my eyes while Yahui gently placed my feet down onto my porch being careful to make sure I was steady before releasing his hold on me. "Thank you, Yahui, for carrying me to the door. And for the most incredible night."

Yahui smiled his eyes roaming over my face, darting from my lips to my eyes then stopping on my, no doubt, disheveled hair. "The honor was and is truly mine, Wu Lihwa... I look forward to many more such memorable dates with you. You are a vision of loveliness to be certain, but you are even more beautiful when you have tousled morning hair, especially when it's from the seat of my Jeep." His voice was playful but sincere. "Shall I pick you up at one? Or did you decide to make it sooner?"

My face flushed with the memory of the conversation we were having before I fell asleep. We were making plans to spend the day together and trying to hammer out the details.

"Umm... What time is it now?"

"It is nearly three am, my Lady," Ayi's stern voice answered "and young Xai Yahui shouldn't be driving anymore tonight. Perhaps he should slumber in one of your many guest bedrooms. Then you can decide on what time to go out after you both get some much-needed sleep."

"Oh, no I could not impose... I will be fi..." Unable to let Yahui place his life at risk when I could insist on him staying here. I interjected. Not wanting him to finish his unwise declaration.

"Your wisdom is endless, Ayi. Of course he must stay." I squeezed his hand tightly. "Could you please show him to the main guest room off in the east wing?" Ayi smiled and nodded, stepping back into the estate so that we could enter. Once inside I turned back to Yahui and gave him a sleepy grin. "Thank you, Yahui for the amazing evening, Happy New Year... and goodnight." I bowed then made to turn and began my trek to the west wing where my bedroom was. I took only half a step before Yahui rushed to stand before me.

"Wu Lihwa, please allow me to return the goodnight wishes to you." Yahui reached his hand up towards my face, gently cradling my cheek in his palm before he stepped closer to me. His lips pressed onto my forehead for a brief kiss, and then I was pulled into his chest. "Good night my sweet Lihwa. May your dreams be half as sweet as you." he lowered his voice into a whisper before adding. "I know I will dream about our New Year's kiss."

My cheeks burned with the memory. We at least where in his dressing room when the clock struck midnight. I could still feel the lingering pressure of his lips on mine. Reluctantly, Yahui released me from his arms and followed Ayi to the guest room to finally get some sleep himself.

My body felt alive with the quivering excitement that Yahui's comment reignited. Before I knew it, I was pushing on my bedroom door just enough to slip in before leaning heavily onto the opposite side with my eyes closed. Unlike before I managed to close the door with little effort. Tracing my fingers over my lips

I allowed myself to imagine that he had kissed me on the lips goodnight instead of my forehead. I was pretty sure that if Ayi hadn't been standing there he very well might have done just that. At least I can dream that he would have anyways.

Fighting with my pea coat I struggled to undress for bed. I heard the door creak open and close shut before I felt warm hands deftly relieving me of the dastardly coats prison.

"Thank you so much, Ayi. I would have been here until next New Year's Eve trying to get that awful thing off by myself." I chuckled and turned to face her. But she wasn't there. The coat was on the chair by my bed but there wasn't anybody in the room with me. The only thing that I found was a scroll of rice paper parchment. Sealed with an all too familiar wax seal and signet.

Without even a second thought to what I was doing I turned and ran to the door. With a flick of my wrist the door flung open and I raced to the east wing desperate to make sure that Yahui was still breathing. For I was absolutely sure that the being who was just in my room would not leave him alive. After all, Longwei would want to ensure that his judgment was carried out correctly this time around.

My feet hardly even touched the floor as I rounded the last hallway before coming to the partially opened guest room door. I could hear Ayi and Yahui conversing, so I slowed down to a normal pace before I entered the room.

"Lihwa," Yahui's voice rang with happiness.

Seeing Yahui's handsome face light up upon seeing me was certainly worth the energy that I had just burned through performing what this era would consider magic. Unfortunately, his happiness was short lived.

"...is everything alright?" He asked just as the room started to spin and my vision began to dim.

I felt the floor rising up to meet me. But just before my body came into contact with it Yahui had me in his arms. Laying me down on the guest bed.

"My Lady!?!" I heard Ayi scream.

Before the world went black and I was transported to a place I never wanted to step foot in ever again in my lifetime. Into a place that I had been condemned to watch the death of my love.

I was standing in the throne room of Longwei. The high lord of the gods, and the look in his golden eyes was enough to make me wish that I had my full array of power available to me, instead of an exhausted and weakened version of my true self. For although I just was able to now use my power, I wasn't quite back to my full capacity. No, nowhere near.

"Zhen'ai, it has been years. Oh wait, what was the name that little human called you? Ah yes. I remember now. *Wu Lihwa.*"

Little human? He means Yahui. My mind raced as I bowed low to Longwei after all he was the ruler of the gods, I was obligated to show my respect even if he had just torn me out of my body. I let my mind race...Trying to fully understand the gravity of me being here while my human body was laying in my guest bed probably with at least two people scared beyond words.

"Zhen'ai, it is nice of you to accept my invitation. I wasn't sure if you would seeing as you have chosen to become a lowly human." His voice echoed throughout the near empty room.

"Invitation? Is that what the scroll was that you left on my bed?" I lowered myself down into a kneeling position. Trying to maintain an air of indifference. Even while my internal thoughts were racing a million miles a minute. "I never got the chance to read it. Seeing as my Lord brought me here without warning." My voice rose in tenor and I could hear it echoing throughout the room. "Were the scrolls contents important?" I smiled. "If so, I will be happy to go back and read it, of course, then when I return..." my sentence was interrupted even if my words still echoed through the room.

"This is such a cavernous space... Isn't it? Do you think that I went a little over the top bringing you here? After all, this place has so much meaning to the two of us... I mean this is the last place that we had spoken with each other." he was deliberately avoiding my question. "Don't you remember?"

Remember? How could I forget. Internally I was raging. While externally I showed no emotion.

"No? Ah, what a shame... well, it was a few thousand years ago... Nevertheless, it is important to keep up with tradition. Especially now that there are such precious few of us left awake." With a flick of his wrist I was floating in midair before landing on a cushion beside his feet on the top of the stairs. "Speaking of being awake, Zhen'ai, do you want to know what woke me up from my restful slumber?"

He paused as I kept my eyes lowered not bothering to fall for his bait. He was trying to get a raise out of me I know, that doesn't mean I have to like it. After all I know the answer... I knew the answer better than anyone else could... The reason he was awake... The thorn in his side that brought him back into this realm of the living was me. No matter how unintentional.

"We need to talk little Zhen'ai," his voice made even the soft pillow I was kneeling on quake. "But you already know that don't you? After all, you are the riddle that answers the riddle that is life isn't that what she used to say?" He was talking like a mad man. I couldn't even fathom who or what he was talking about... Yet his next words proved to be more than I could take. "I think that I shall keep you here with me."

My eyes hardened and flashed up to meet his gaze. No matter how much I knew I wasn't supposed to. No matter how many laws I was now adding to my list of broken ones... I couldn't remain here. I needed to get back to Yahui.

"Ah, there is my favorite granddaughter, I knew she had to be in there somewhere." he laughed bending down and flicking his finger into the center of my forehead.

"Don't let Neihwa hear you say that, grandfather," I said, the venom in my voice evident. "Oh wait, she never will for you banished her from ever returning home. Yet me." I took in a large breath. "Me. You can't just let me be happy. Your favorite granddaughter you say. You force me to watch as you murder the man I love, forbidding him to ever reincarnate again, yet I am your favorite?"

"And yet, he has, has he not? Which brings us full circle." Longwei grabbed a knife that sat on an offering plate. His cold eyes inspecting the blade. He twirled it over in his hand before he used its tip to clean a speck of dirt from the nail of his index finger's. "Humans are such amusing playthings. It was so easy to bend his thoughts and play with his weaknesses. Well mostly..." Longwei's eyes glared down at me, no longer interested in the speck of dirt that was now on the end of his blade. "He is very strong willed when it comes to you... Why is that I wonder? Hmmm, no matter..." He smiled. His gold eyes burned with malice. "Do tell me what you thought of my little gift?"

"What gift was that, My Lord?" I spit out the last two words, wishing that I too had a knife in hand...

"Oh, dear me. I thought that you would enjoy my little special effects at your little human's concert. The smoke was just the right touch, don't you agree?" Longwei motions were a blur, His hand held the knife below my chin making me look up into his eyes. "The right touch to make you remember the full range of my power over your dear mortal's life. I concede that there is something different about this one isn't there? This lifetime's reincarnation of Su Yang has sparked a great interest in me." His laughter resounded throughout the cavernous space. Sounding like the thunder that we had heard twice last night. "You know that even now he is attempting to save your life. Though he knows not that you are in no direct danger." Longwei retracted the blade from my neck. "At least not from me. Perhaps from the Doctors."

"Doctors?" I growled.

"Oh yes... He carried your soulless body to the hospital. Even with Ayi's anger flaring. Now that is a woman...She is a wild cat, I bet she would rival all the high priestesses that have ever served me. I am willing to bet she would *serve* me well."

"Your hypocritical ways are no longer viewed as gospel in this time Longwei."

"Hypocritical? My you have grown a larger vocabulary. Where have you ever learned such a word? It doesn't matter, Zhen'ai. You will obey me. You all will obey me."

His eyes glanced over to a large mural on the opposite wall. A family portrait of sorts, depicting all of the ethereal court. All of the gods and goddesses. No matter their station were represented. Even my parents and myself.

I remained silent as I reached out my mind to Ayi. Hoping that I had enough time to tell her to get my body and Yahui out of the hospital. I needed to be back at the estate, in my room, when I returned to my body. For I fully intended to be back in my body soon.

Longwei, for all his immense power and authority, had forgotten one very important rule of the lesser gods. In his arrogance he forgot, that in bringing me here, and not just to this room, but to sit by his feet. He gave me the one thing that would place us on more level grounds.

When I first was ripped out of my body I had very little power... So little, in fact, that had he left me in my body I probably would never have regain it at all. Now. Now he was making all of my power return.

While I might have been the reason for his awakening, he was the power supply for my extremely depleted *battery*. And in this brief encounter, I was now one hundred percent charged.

Chapter 16

No, I don't know what happened. One moment she is talking to me the next she is unresponsive laying on a bed." Yahui ran his hand through his hair pacing the waiting room hallway of the local hospital. He had driven Lihwa's unconscious body here after a heated argument with her caretaker and butler/chauffeur. Ayi was adamant that Lihwa would be alright she just needed rest. Yet Yahui felt that there was something more serious going on. Part of him was wishing that he had listened to Ayi.

"I gently lifted her back into my arms for the third time in three hours and brought her here to the hospital. Haku, that was three hours ago. And they are refusing to let me go back there with her." A door opened down the long corridor and a familiar face strode into view. Though she didn't appear to be at all happy. Her gaze was a steely as her hair, and regardless of her age she was able to traverse the long hallway with a speed and agility of a woman at least half her age.

"Do you know how long it took for us to find you?" Her voice cut Yahui to the bone. Her fear for her lady was evident.

"Haku, I need to go." Yahui hung up with Haku and dropped to his knees before his elder. "Ayi, I know that you are angry with me... and that I don't deserve your forgiveness. But I only..."

"You only brought her here because of your fear for her safety. I know that Xai Yahui. But I am here to take her back home where she will stay. She.... She.... Um, my Lady hates hospitals. That is a story that isn't mine to tell. You will just have to inquire her reasons once she wakes up." Ayi, wrung her hands together nervously. "Where is the Doctor? The receptionist said she was going to call him and have him meet me here."

"I haven't seen a doctor in hours. Not since I brought her here. When I brought her in, I gave the Doctor a report of what had happened and then they rushed her through those swinging doors." Yahui motioned toward a pair of black and stainless-steel doors.

"Through there you say?" Ayi asked.

Yahui nodded his response his eyes still looking down at his knees. He remained still kneeling by Ayi's feet.

"Then through there we shall go and collect my Lady," she stated, walking towards the swinging doors.

§

Yahui shook his head once again in awe of the sheer audacity of the woman sitting on a chair by the head of Wu Lihwa's bed. When Ayi marched into the exam room and demanded that the doctors release Lihwa, he wished that he had the foresight to have recorded the exchange. Yahui's original opinion of Ayi was proving to be more than accurate. She may seem sweet and fragile. But she is anything but, especially when it comes to her Lady.

Yahui let his eyes fix on the very creature to whom Ayi would give her life for, for whom she would tear the very fabric of the world apart to bring home safely. Wu Lihwa, a woman that in less than a week's time had made him feel the complete gambit of emotions. From the second that he saw her she made his heart dictate what his mind, his body and his soule would do.

With a light touch Yahui moved a stray strand of hair from her face. Tucking it in behind her ear, Yahui sighed at the intriguing smile that played on her lips. Even though Lihwa still hadn't woken up her skin color was already returning to normal. She was looking so much better once Ayi had him tuck Lihwa back into her own bed. He should have listened in the first place. But hindsight is always twenty/twenty.

He needed to get some sleep himself. He couldn't remember when he last was asleep. He knew that he hadn't had much over the past six days. Although the time spent with Lihwa was well worth the missed hours of rest. Still his eyelids felt like rocks were tied to them he just didn't want to leave Lihwa's side.

"Xai Yahui. You must rest. Watching her isn't going to make her wake up any faster. I promise to wake you the moment that she is conscious." Even though she hadn't slept either Ayi appeared to be determined to make Yahui head to bed.

"Yes, I know a watched pot doesn't boil. I will head to bed and I would be most grateful to you in waking me up the moment she is conscious." Yahui stood up grasping Lihwa's hand and bringing it to his lips. Before replacing it at her side on the bed.

Turning swiftly on his heels and with shoulders back he exited the room making his way to the guest room.

It seemed like the hallway was lengthening with each step that he took. But after what seemed like forever, he found himself closing the guest room's door.

Exhaustion won over, and not even bothering to strip out of his clothes Yahui collapsed onto the bed and was soon fast asleep.

Chapter 17

hundreds of needles were stabbing me all at once, followed by the sensation that my limbs were made of lead. For neither my hands nor my feet wanted to move the moment that I entered back into my physical body. I heard Ayi order Yahui to bed, and no matter how much I wanted to see him and talk to him. The first thing I needed to do was talk to Ayi about our dire security need. For we were certainly needing to beef up our *security here at the estate...* and I wasn't talking about security cameras and hiring an army of bodyguards. Well, not yet anyway.

We needed the assistance of one of the temples most sacred secrets. A ward to keep all other gods out. Also, I needed an amulet to give to Yahui if I was to protect him too, he couldn't stay here all the time after all.

"You care to explain what is going on? Or do you want me to guess?" Ayi walked to the dresser pouring two glasses of water. Before returning to the bed. "Because I think I am going to need a stronger drink, my Lady, if who I think is behind all of this morning's excitement is in fact Longwei."

All I had to do was look at Ayi and she brought one of the glasses to her lips downing the content before passing me the other one. "I cannot go into full details with you Ayi, but you are correct. And it is sufficient to say that Longwei has awoken and we are the largest blip on his radio."

"Radar, my Lady. The saying is a 'Blip on his Radar.'" Ayi stared into her empty glass for several moments before turning her concerned eyes to me. "Do you fear that Longwei will once again kill your love?"

Biting my lip, I regarded my true feelings. It was strange that Longwei hadn't already tried to attack him. I mean he had already toyed with him. Yahui's actions at the venue when we first arrived now made perfect sense. He wasn't himself. Longwei was attempting to make him leave me? Or me leave him? But he didn't try to kill him like he had done before. And he had plenty of opportunities. It was clear from just the first few words out of Longwei's mouth that he had spoken to Yahui. For that is where he learned my human name. But the meeting I had with Longwei was odd, infuriating, oh yes he made me madder than I had ever felt before in my existence, but nonetheless odd. And I still felt like there was something very important that I was missing. But was I afraid for my love's life?

"Yes! I fear that something may happen to Yahui. Though I do not know what Longwei is up to. That is why I need you to go to Meihui's temple and procure for me a protection amulet. Grab as many as you can. One for yourself and for Nia as well.

I don't want him to take you from me anymore than I want my love wiped off the face of this earth."

I reached my hand over to Ayi's empty glass and with the slightest touch filled it for her with huangjiu. Ayi's eyes widened. "My Lady?"

"Drink that Ayi... It will help to calm your resolve. My dear Ayi. I am not as weak as I was at the beginning of this ordeal. You know that I was drained of all my powers when I had awoken... But now Longwei has, unknowingly perhaps, been the cause of my total renewal of strength. I'm also completely sure he is regretting that now."

Ayi gulped down the strong huangjiu before speaking again. "I'll get right on the ward before I go to the temple. I'll wake Nia to take me. Will you require me to wake up."

"Leave waking up Yahui to me, Ayi." I couldn't hide the smile on my lips as I said these words. Nor had I missed the knowing smile that graced Ayi's face when she rose and headed for the door.

"Stay safe my Lady," she added, and with a small bow of her head, she left me to my thoughts.

∫

I waited until I heard the sound of tires on gravel fading down the driveway before exiting my chambers. I had changed out of my nightgown into a pair of skinny blue jeans and a red linen blouse that had billowing sleeves and a laced-up bodice. My intricate hairstyle was a product of magic. Though I was sure that had Ayi stayed she could have done my hair up with the same attention to detail. I didn't chastise myself to harshly for the use of it.

My newly regained powers hummed in this form. Yet they weren't unruly, as I had expected them to be. Well had I awoken with them anyways...

Prior to heading for the door, I noticed I had a faint radiant glow when I checked my reflection in the mirror, not too noticeable, just enough to make my skin and eyes appear healthy. I had spent the better part of a day unconscious after all, and if I wanted him to take me out, then I had to appear in good health. At least this was my thought as I stood outside the guest bedroom door.

Hesitating briefly before I opened the door, turning the knob slowly I began pushing the door open to find Yahui passed out cold on the bed. He lay there sprawled out still fully dressed above the covers with even the guest slippers still on his feet. His eyes were puffy and there were dark circles there, from lack of sleep, no doubt. What kind of girlfriend would I be if I beamed of health while my love looked like he hadn't slept in weeks?

I sighed lightly before closing my eyes and when I opened them I was no longer dressed for a date, but outfitted to stay at home. My hair was still up but instead of the intricate up do, a messy bun took its place. My jeans and blouse where now a pair of yoga pants and a spaghetti strap tank top that bore a drawing of an anime character with bunny ears and a cute phrase that stated that "*some bunny luvs me.*"

Feeling more adequately dressed, I strolled over to the bed and removed the slippers from his feet. His toes curled in response. I smiled warmly while I placed them on the floor next to the bed, positioned so he could easily slide them on once he woke up. He is so adorable when he is sleeping, regardless of the fact that he was in desperate need of the rest. He needed to be higher in the bed, I decided, and with a gentle breath blown over my lips Yahui was lifted up and deposited gently down on the bed with his head cradled in the soft pillow instead of being pressed into the rough fabric of the woven comforter. Pleased with the way that he was positioned I headed to the wardrobe pulling out a plush blanket and I preceded in covering him up. He moved a little from the attention, wrapping his arms around the soft fabric and bringing it to his face. The sweetest smile graced his lips and I felt my breath catch.

I was no stranger to watching over my love, no, I have watched over him in all his reincarnations. Honestly, people of this age would probably look at me as a stalker, I laughed leaving the door open slightly as I went to the kitchen to see about getting *breakfast*. I'm sure that cook must be awake by now.

∫

Thirty minutes later I walked into the guest bedroom carrying a tray with breakfast for two. Stuffed steamed buns filled a large serving bowl and a bowl for each of us of rice porridge. A teapot and two cups sat in the center of the heavy tray, while I had no problem carrying it, I couldn't help but appreciate the hard work that Ayi and cook did every day.

Yahui was still curled up on the bed sound asleep. I walked to the small stand that was over in the far corner next to a high window that overlooked the snow-covered garden and pond. Setting the tray down I began to pour myself a cup of tea. A mumbled sleepy voice sounded behind me, at first I couldn't make out the words that Yahui was mumbling. But the sound of his voice was so groggy and low it ignited a warm feeling inside of me. But when he spoke again that changed.

It happened so slowly, like you sometimes see on TV. The teapot slipped from my fingers, tumbling sideways the handcrafted lid slipped off giving the hot tea free reign to flow not only from the spout but from this much larger opening. The liquid splashed onto the teak hardwood flooring and on the slippers that covered my bare feet. If it had burned my flesh I did not care, nor did I care that the floor was now covered in tea and broken shards of pottery.

I pivoted on my warm, wet toes, turning to Yahui... The man who was my world, the man who just over thirty-five hours ago promised to court me. Me. Wu Lihwa. And I hoped to always remain his. Except when I gazed upon this man who now, instead of laying curled up in the blanket, sat on the edge of the bed. I knew that something was not right.

I knew it from the cadence of his voice, I knew it from the confused look that was painted over every one of his handsome features on his face. But most of all I knew it by the words that he had already said and was now moving his perfect lips to say again.

"Zhen'ai, it's you isn't it? Zhen'ai, my goddess. Where have you brought me? Where are my men?" He stood and closed the short distance between us with two of his long purposeful strides. His hands slid over my cheeks cradling my face in his tender hands, his eyes searched mine looking for the answers to his questions yet it seemed that his search had only made yet another question, one that seemed to trouble him more so than the rest.

"Zhen'ai, what happened to your beautiful eyes?"

Damn you Longwei!!!!

Chapter 18

Of all the atrocities that I had imagined Longwei committing to my love. Never had I dreamed that he would stoop to doing this. Of all the godly abilities that were at his disposal, Longwei the High Lord of the Gods had to choose the one unforeseen act that I knew not how to correct.

It had been three hours since *Yahui* had awakened... It was Yahui's body, per se, although that fact was rendered irrelevant...

Because the soule of the man who had gazed at me from his rigid position by the window, was most definitely that of Wu Xia.

Out of all his questions, it had been easy to respond to two. Was it really me, Zhen'ai, who stood before him? Yes, yes I am she/ And the eye color. I was able to fix that as well. Thankfully, that magic was as simple as changing my clothes and the way that my hair looked. Explaining the rest. That was proving to be a bit of a chore. For try as I might he didn't understand why he was here. And honestly besides the obvious fact that Longwei was a spiteful god. I couldn't give him an answer, at least not one that he was satisfied with.

Wu Xia stared out the window, his brow furrowed making a crease in his (Yahui's) normally smooth forehead. He had been poised there, arms crossed, silent never once looking at me at least not that I had seen him look, since I had given him the truthful answers to his heart wrenching questions.

Yes, he had moved certainly, for he was of course breathing. I had seen his hand stroke the smooth glass twice and he even touched the light fabric of the curtains a few times. But I had not seen him look at me since I told him that his men were all dead. And that he had died with them.

"I remember dying," his voice finally broke the unnerving silence. "I remember dying in your arms. Although..." His eyes finally rested on me, full of sadness and some small flickers of doubt, but his eyes sought mine while he dropped his arms to his sides. "You are human now and back then you were not. I remember. I remember your tears. And I remember the mournful cry that filled my ears and made me see you standing there from once you weren't."

I stood, I wanted to be once again holding him, but he held up a hand stopping me, it was a warning for me to wait....

He wasn't ready for my nearness. Not yet, and I feared perhaps not ever.

"You cried out that you loved me. Are these still your feelings?" his face softened, and he took a tentative step towards me. I stood stark still before him. Afraid to move although my insides were already churning in a hurricane force storm of emotions.

"Yes, Wu Xia, I love you... I have always loved you... In whatever lifetime you have appeared..."

"Even this one, this one where I am not a warrior with honor and power but a man who performs in front of crowds singing and dancing like some Emperor's fool?" his voice was tight and cross.

"Yes, I love this lifetime's you as well. And he is a warrior. Not only in the since of being in the army, at least he used to be in the army... But he is also a warrior in the game as well... And he is no fool, Xia. Nor does he get treated as such. He is adored and held in extremely high regard. Exactly in the same respect that you were held all those years ago..."

"Two thousand two hundred and thirty-six years ago?" his voice broke as he took yet another step forward.

"Well yes, Xia, give or take a few months... It has been many, many lifetimes since your soule has walked this earth." my heart was pounding in my chest. He was so close, yet I still didn't dare move.

Closing the distance completely Xia stood before me. If I was to reach out my hand it would come to rest on his chest. Standing at full attention his body was solid, his stance firm, there was nothing off with his posture at all... Yahui was in peak fitness. Wu Xia might believe Yahui was a fool. Yet, he must know the facts all prove that Yahui is not a weakling, far from it.

"Zhen'ai, goddess of my ancestors, my beautiful goddess, who has captured my heart. Why?" his voice quiet, though his eyes were liquid fire. I felt the heat of his glance and then the warmth of his body. His hand slid up over my neck traveling further up before stopping at the thin stretchy cord that held my hair up into this bun. His fingers worked with skill and his mission was clear once my hair cascaded down over my shoulders.

Once he was satisfied with the way my hair looked, His arms engulfed me pulling me tight to him.

"Zhen'ai, my Goddess. Why did you only now choose to become mortal? All those nights I lay alone thinking about you. Wanting to hold you in my mortal arms instead of only in my dreams." His eyes long fully searched mine. I could feel the heat of his gaze burning into me. His lips opened and my own eyes were unable to look anywhere else.

"We walked together in the dreamscape, so many nights, yet not until my death did you choose to come to me. Only in my death did you decide to change. What was it that made you this way? Was it to be his?"

What? He thinks that I did what? Pressing my hands fully onto his chest I pushed myself away so that I could see his face fully. I needed him to see mine as well. His eyes still smoldered. His lips parted slightly before they made their descent, on a collision course straight for mine. I've wanted to be right here, in his arms, with him wanting me, desiring me, in every way, shape, and form.

"Wu Xia, Stop!" My voice rang out through the room. His eyes grew wide, I guess I hadn't only surprised myself.

"Stop? Why on earth should I stop? Zhen'ai, I am a man, a strong virile man. You are a woman. A very beautiful woman," lowering his eyes, taking me all in, stopping at the swelling of my breasts through the fabric of my tank top. He lunged for my waist pulling me toward him again. His voice full of raw emotion, he lowered his lips to my ear. "Zhen'ai, it is you whose body is on display for the whole world to see. We have lain together in dreams, oh so many nights. Why should I stop when I can have you now, here, and we can both finally experience the release that we have been craving?" His breath sent wave upon wave of heat through me.

I couldn't deny that his words were true. But I couldn't be with him either. I couldn't lay with Wu Xia. No. Not while Yahui was locked up somewhere in that body. It wasn't right, on so many different levels. I knew this... I knew this to be true, but I also knew that with one kiss my resolve would be gone. I would lose myself in the passion of his kiss. I had to leave. I had to put some distance between us, I had to stop him. Stop him without either one of us losing control.

And in that moment, I could think of only one way to achieve that outcome. And so, without a single word of warning, not even a hint of my coming action. I did just that.

Chapter 19

Y ou did what!?!" Ayi's voice rang through the estate
once I met her at the door upon her return and began
to explain how my morning had gone. "I placed him
into a deep slumber." I frowned looking down at my
hands.

"You knocked him out you mean..." exasperation poured
from Ayi. Sighing she walked past me towards the east wing.
Where Yahui's body and Wu Xia's soule lay on the guest bed. "My
Lady, I'm sure that you had just cause, but I don't think that Xai
Yahui will appreciate you rendering him unconscious."

"Ayi... I think that Yahui would be pleased that I had done
just that." I rushed after her. Stopping at the open door while Ayi
went over to the bed to examine Yahui's unconscious body. I still

hadn't told her the full reason why I knocked him out.

"Oh? I am curious to hear just why Xai Yahui would be pleased that his girlfriend knocked him out?" Ayi bent low checking his pulse. Satisfied that he was in fact still alive she rounded on me. I always knew that Ayi was an imposing woman. But never had I ever been the subject of her full displeasure. "Well? I'm waiting."

"Ayi, please sit down, and I will tell you exactly why..."

§

It took nearly an hour to completely describe the events of the morning. I even had to take time to explain the reason why my eyes were still the color of cherry blossoms instead of the usual amber, which in all reality, I had completely forgotten. Remedying that, at least, made Ayi sit quietly for the remainder of my explanation.

"So, you see, I either had to submit to the desires of the flesh, with a man I know has long been dead... And in doing so being unfaithful to my Yahui. Or render him unconscious while I tried to figure out a way to reverse whatever it is that Longwei did to Yahui." I paused, looking at the stoic expression on Ayi's face before I continued. "Were you able to acquire the amulets?"

It was like those words woke Ayi from her silence. She pulled a piece of rolled up silk from her pocket and held it towards me. "I was able to purchase three. But the high priestess told me that the fourth was not for sale but a gift. I was grateful for the boon when we left there, but now I am more weary that even these amulets won't be enough."

"Grandmother? Grandmother?" Nia called down the hall. "You forgot this in the car. It's addressed to Zhen'ai."

Forgetting to grab the amulets I raced to Nia. I had the envelope in my hand breaking the seal before Ayi could even get up from her seat. Much like how I had known who the scroll was from on my bed by the seal. This one's lotus flower signet was unmistakable as well. When I had sent Ayi to the temple, I never would have guessed that the Goddess herself would in turn send me a message. Meihui's delicate handwriting flowed over the paper. The magic in the message that only my eyes could read.

Dear Zhen'ai,

I can hardly imagine the pain that you are feeling. Once I sense the presence of Wu Xia, I nearly wept for I know the torment that this will bring. When I offered to help you become human, I feared that father, Longwei, would awaken but I had never thought that he would stoop to this level in order to maintain his unjustifiable decree.

I can only hope that this gets to you in time to stop you from consummating a relationship with Wu Xia. For to do so would have dire consequences for not only you, but for the souls of your beloveds.

Forgive me, dear Zhen'ai, for not delivering this message to you in person. I had tried, but found your residence shrouded in a ward that I could not pass. I will head west to the temple of Yuanjun. Out of all of us that are awake, the Queen is the most likely to know of a way to reverse this wrong.

Stay strong my dear Zhen'ai... I will be in contact with you again soon.

Meihui

The fourth amulet is for Yahui to wear. It will help to bring the spirits together, other than that I don't know what else to do. I wish that I could do more. Watch for my letter by the full moon. We both know that I will have to endure the trials in order to talk with Yuanjun. Do not lose hope. For hope is the light in the darkness, a pathway to where true happiness is found.

Ayi pulled out the fourth amulet, handing it to me. Her eyes were still leery, gazing over to the man lying on the bed. "You think this will work, my Lady?"

"I hope so Ayi... Like the letter said, all I can do is hope." I could feel the magic within the amulet. It pulsed like a beating heart in my hand. With determined steps I strode to the bed, bending over my love's body I placed the ornate jade amulet around his neck.

The instant that the cord was bound the magic coursed through Yahui's body, His arms flailed out grabbing either side of the full-sized mattress while his back arched high off the bed. Tears formed in my eyes, glistening gems proving just who I really was. After what seemed like hours, Yahui's body relaxed and I placed my hand over his heart feeling the beating as if it were my own. Thankful that it was still there.

"Yahui, if you can hear me, my love. Come back to me. Find my light in the darkness. I will be there searching for you." I whispered. Leaning down I kissed his forehead, much like he had done to me not that long ago. I closed my eyes repeating my words in that of a silent prayer.

My lone tear released from its confines of my eye made its way downward. Following a well-worn trail down my cheek towards the cause of its formation. For it seemed I had cried more so for this man then any god or goddess had ever cried for a mortal. It glistened as it fell, catching the light that filtered in from the nearby window. Landing in the corner of Yahui's mouth it faltered there teetering on the edge of his upper lip. For a second it glowed pure white before falling over into the small opening between Yahui's lips, and in an instant was gone.

"What? What was that, my Lady?" Ayi gasped, her voice was high and frantic... "What was that light?"

Ayi's called made me open my eyes. I searched my love's face but found nothing changed.

"I do not know... I didn't see a light. My eyes were closed, and I blocked everything out." My eyes sought out Ayi's and she was standing now her eyes locked behind me. She was silent and I felt my patience wane.

Ayi was my right hand. Always present when needed and always had the uncanny ability to anticipate my needs before I even knew them. Looking at her shocked form made my body turn cold Something was wrong, this was not the Ayi I had grown to know.

Ayi raised her shaking hand, pointing at the wall behind me, and I turned to see a mural forming on the once bare wall. A beautiful scene of a temple, one of my temples actually. The likeness of it was incredible, it was a glimpse into a much different lifetime. And I recognized it at once. It was the place where Su Yang stole my heart.

Chapter 20

My body began to tremble uncontrollably, my tremors came in terrible crashing waves. Wave after wave of uncontrollable spasms rendering me immobile.

It couldn't be... But yet it was... My thoughts raced. It was the place that this all began. *"Why?"* I sobbed. As I watched the magical painting form a figure. A man. It was hazy without detail, just a mass of brilliant color in a dense fog. Yet I knew who it was an answer to my prayer. As quickly as the painting had begun, it stopped, and with it the room faded to black.

"Wu Lihwa... I hear you..."

§

For the second time I felt my soule being torn from my body by the order of Longwei. To say that this particular power of his to summon any of us to him whenever he wished, was well loved by the rest of us gods and goddesses. Would be the biggest lie I would have ever told. We hated it. It was Longwei who loved it. Yet when I appeared in his presence, I was surprised that we stood only meters outside my own property. His eyes glared from the obvious impenetrable ward and back to me in rapid succession.

"Zhen'ai, did you think that I couldn't reach you if you placed that thing around your estate? Or did you think I wouldn't be able to touch your precious little mortal?" His eyes lightened and a horrible smile broke the surface of his face. Making me shiver once. Even without my body I was still being plagued by these annoyances.

"How is he doing, anyway? Enjoying his new roommates? Or are they really the old ones and he is in fact the new?" he scoffed a billowing laugh erupted from him. Causing the ground to shake. You and my daughter are working together... I wondered who taught you the spell to turn human. Now it is blatantly obvious." He let out a thunderous breath... Be wary of gifts that seem to have no price. Granddaughter. Or you will come to wish you had stayed in my throne room."

"What are you playing at Longwei? Why are you doing this?" My fists clenched as I glared at him. I felt my hair start to rise around me filled with the static of the electricity I felt coursing through me.

"Zhen'ai, do you really want to cross me again? Look at the punishment you received for leaving my presence without my permission last time. Do you really want to chance what will happen if you displease me yet again?"

"Are you saying you did horrible things to Yahui, filling his head with his past lives, because I left your throne room without asking permission? Are you a child or a god? For you are acting like a child... Doling out punishments when you are displeased or not attended to." I could see the displease in Longwei's eyes. But I could not stem the flow of my ill-advised words. "You stole me from my body then and you did it again just now. With your actions as my model... What punishment should I dole out to you?"

"Watch your tongue. You are nothing but a lesser goddess. A plaything that we allow to exist. Remember that Granddaughter. As you attempt to sort out the jumbled mess that lies trapped in that poor boy's head... For you will need it. I am not the only one who doesn't want you with that human. But I may just be the only one of us who doesn't want to lose you in the process. Remember that, Zhen'ai! Be gone!!"

I couldn't respond before feeling my spirit flying through the air, I woke up in my body still trembling from head to toe. This time not only from shock but from a deep-seated anger.

Standing I ran to the bed. My shaking hands pressed into the sides of Yahui's handsome face.

"Wake up. Arise Yahui!" I screamed- evoking my magic and reversing my former spell. I watched as his eyes fluttered open. A light of recognition lit there in his gaze.

"Lihwa, thank the gods you are alright."

Yahui. It was Yahui. I should have been thrilled but Longwei's words still echoed in my mind and before I could stop myself. I blurted out:

"How many of you are in there?"

∫

The high pitch whistle of the teakettle brought Ayi to her feet. She had asked the cook to go shopping and gave her a list of items that Ayi knew would take her a while to acquire. Over half of the items on the list we had no need of. But Ayi listed them anyways.

"The kitchen table was the perfect place to talk about impossible things." Ayi had said shortly after the cook had left and we all ambled to the table sitting in a circle. All eyes rested on me.

Out of everyone sitting there it was Yahui's eyes that stared at me expectantly. Watching me, waiting for me to explain. I couldn't meet his gaze. I looked at my hands resting on the table, looked at the way my skin stretched over muscles, tendons and bone. When I could no longer find interest in my hands I looked at the wood of the table... Anywhere but at those eyes that were looking at me, I was sure that they were not filled with love, but with suspicion, anger, hurt, and quite possibly hate. For he should hate me. He should hate me for loving him, and in loving him condemning him to this wretched situation that he found himself in.

Longwei said that this was all my doing. And for once in my long life I started to believe that he was right.

"Don't everyone speak at once," Ayi called over her shoulder from the counter where she made our tea. "The gods know I wouldn't want to miss a single word."

Nia snickered at his Grandmother's attempt to break the growing tension that hung in the air between us all. Sighing heavily, I dared a glance at Yahui. His soft brown eyes watched me looking at me with wonder and I couldn't bear to see him looking at me like that, to see the love actually there hurt me more.

"Why don't you hate me?" I whispered. My voice trembled much like the rest of my body. Yahui shook his head. Slowly at first and then he stood up rounding the table as Ayi turned with the tray of tea heavy in her arms.

"Ayi. I need to speak with your lady. In private! We will be back for tea once we are done." Taking my hand in his Yahui dragged me through the vacant hallways up into the guest room that we had moments ago left. Stopping only when we stood in front of the magically painted mural. His eyes gazed long and hard at it. With his free hand he ran a finger down the walkway that leads from the temple to a stream. Turning to meet my gaze he spoke.

"The water from this stream tastes of Orange blossoms after it rains. And these trees," he indicated the cherry trees in the foreground. "I planted them. I planted them for you."

"Yahui?" I whispered. He turned and looked at me. His eyes shining with newly formed tears.

"Lihwa. It is me. I am Xia Yahui. But that is not all of who I am, nor how could I be. That is what you meant when you asked me, isn't it? Lihwa, I remember all of my lives. But I remember that you are not only an amazing woman but you are a goddess as well. Zhen'ai. It was you who came to me in my dream. Why didn't you tell me?"

Chapter 21

Y ahui, I didn't tell you because it wasn't a dream. It was real. It was IRL..." I looked down at our hands clasped together. My body still shook uncontrollably making me want to sit down and curl up into a ball with my knees pressed into my chest, like I had done before.

"So, we are alone here. Mind telling me why I should hate you?" Yahui asked, his free hand moving to caress my cheek. His eyes were warm and inviting. So much like Su Yang.

Realization dawned on me and I pulled my hand from his grasp.

"You should hate me because I am the reason that your lives have been plagued. I am the reason that Wu Xia died in battle that day. It was my punishment. Now, now you stand here, with all your past lives occupying your head. It is a punishment to me. For loving you. My selfishness. You would be better off to hate me, to hate me and let me fade away." With each word I trembled more until my whole body shook while I sobbed.

Yahui, wrapped his arms around me holding my shaking body tightly to him. I struggled at first trying to get away yet Yahui just held me tighter. Letting my tears hit the floor. Each sounding louder than the next.

Looking down at the floor Yahui chuckled. "So, is this how you could afford such a beautiful estate. By crying rare gems?" Yahui laughed even louder. "If making you sad will bring us a fortune maybe we should be thanking Longwei, instead of fearing him."

"You know not what you say. It is unwise to mock him." *And unwise to mock the unknown individual as well.* I thought thinking again on Longwei's words. I sniffled gazing up to meet Yahui's eyes.

"Then we shall find a way to be happy. A life that we should have had many lifetimes ago. For I may have lived many lives. But there is one constant in each. And that is I have always loved you. And if that is wrong. Then I don't want to be right." Yahui cupped my chin in his hand bringing my eyes back up to his before he let his lips cover mine, for the second time. This time the raw emotions of everything that had happened fueled the kiss and I purred into his lips.

All too soon it felt like a kiss that was transcending many lifetimes. I could sense the soules of so many of Yahui's past lives. The power of that kiss was immense, and that power was growing. I was trembling harder know than I had before but this time it wasn't from anger. And it seemed that I wasn't the only one.

Yahui fell back onto the bed. His body began to spasm and his hands flew up to clutch the sides of his head.

"Oh gods! I guess that the answer to your question from before is many. Dear Zhen'ai. There are so many in here," he added, pointing to his head.

"Yahui???" With all the emotions and questions flowing through me that was the only word I could think to say. I was so scared, and yet angry that we had stopped kissing. Which only made me more mad at myself. *I am killing him.* But my thoughts were interrupted by Yahui's pain-filled voice.

"I can feel two very vocal past lives. The others are content to sit back and watch. But Yang and Xia? Not so much," Yahui laid back on the bed. Still holding his head between his hands. Breathing heavily, he closed his eyes.

§

While my love lay there in immense pain. I sat on the floor watching him. All Longwei's words continued to echo through my brain. But they were making no sense.

Shaking my head to try and shake off his words I began to contemplate the most troublesome problem. The problem of Yahui's new roommates.

It was evident from my earlier run in with Wu Xia that the past lives could come out when Yahui slept. Or more specifically, when he woke up. Which meant that every time from now until we figure out a way of removing those added soules we stood the chance of having a different past life rearing their head every morning. Or after any sleep. *Could it happen after a nap?* My eyes racked over the still form of Yahui as he lay there still breathing heavily. I let my energy flow over him, and I still felt the strong presence of Yahui. I let out a long breath that I hadn't even realized I was holding. At least I knew that he could rest his eyes without worry. But how long until that was no longer an option. I needed to take away that chance. And the only way that I could think of to do that was to take away the possibility of Yahui falling asleep.

∫

I'm unsure how long the throbbing headache lasted for Yahui but when it had finally stopped Yahui found me on my knees in front of him on the floor peering up at him. Concern evident on my face.

"We need to talk. I believe I understand what is happening. But I will have to wait until I hear back from Meihui. Yahui, I have a question that I must ask of you. You can refuse, yet I think that you will want to seriously consider this."

"Your eyes, they are once again a beautiful pale pink. The color of the cherry blossoms. So beautiful. Ask me the question," he sighed.

"How would you feel about not sleeping, at least until we get this all sorted?" I tried to give an innocent grin but failed miserably.

"There is something that you're not telling me," Yahui sighed. "What happens when I go to sleep?"

"Well, I'm not one hundred percent sure, but I think that when you go to sleep, there is a huge possibility that you will wake up as one of your past lives. And well, it's already the third of January, and we have the test filming in two days. I don't know

[156]

what they would do if you, well, if you weren't you." I placed my hand on Yahui's cheek. His skin was so soft, and he smiled.

Leaning into my warm touch he shook his head. "I will need to talk to Haku, it's the third you say. I bet my phone has blown up."

"No, it's still in one piece. I put it on your nightstand."

Yahui laughed clasping my hand in his so that I couldn't move away. "Now I understand why you don't get some of the terms that people use. I meant that I bet my phone has a lot of messages, both text and voicemail. I haven't talked to Haku since the afternoon of the first. Oh no. My mother."

"Ah, I see. So not blown up into pieces just blown up with information." Smiling I consider this then add: "I get it. And I think my phone may have blown up as well, seeing as I haven't touched it since the 27th."

Yahui leaned his head down to rest on top of mine before whispering, "Lihwa, I love you."

I expected to feel the transformations completion. His words should have done the trick. But nothing had changed. "I think that you believe that you love me. But Yahui, my handsome Yahui, I think that you won't know how you actually feel about me, until you are free from the influences of all your past lives and their feelings for me." I kissed his cheek then winked at him. "Besides I want to hear you sing that line to me up on stage. You still owe me a date." I thumped his nose with my index finger and headed for the door.

"Do you really think that if I went to sleep right now that I would wake up as one of my past lives?" Yahui asked peering over the top of his cell phone's screen at me.

"I know that it has already happened once. And it took me knocking him out to keep him from taking me to bed." I walked out of the room, leaving him there to let that information stew. It didn't take long before he had raced out the door and had caught up with me grabbing my wrist in his hand.

"Which one?" his eyes probed mine.

"Which one do you think?"

"Wu Xia?" his voice was flat. "It was him, wasn't it. He has very strong feelings for you. And the way that your eyes look right now make him, and Yang for that matter, want to take you into my arms. I'm sorry, Lihwa," his head bowed low, looking at the floor.

"Don't apologize. It wasn't you, so it's not your apology that I need or that I will accept." His eyes searched my face.

"So, how are you going to keep me awake and still have me in working condition?" Yahui waves his phone in the air. "Haku expects the both of us at his place in the morning. Or he says there will be hell to pay, and I believe him."

"Sounds like between your Haku and my Ayi we have a formidable pair of caretakers."

"Caretaker? Don't let Haku hear you call him that. He might start to think that he has to watch over me more. I think right now I will not be needing his extra scrutiny." He laughed.

"True. Much like how I placed your body into a deep slumber. I can do just the opposite. Where I can make it so you don't need to sleep. There is a time limit. Two weeks. That is all I can do at one time. And then you will have to sleep. Hopefully when Meihui messages me at the full moon. In a week's time she will have a way to reverse this curse." I bit my lip gazing over Yahui's face. Taking in the line of his jaw and the slope of his nose. When he is pouting like he is now, he looks so innocent and sweet. I just want to eat him up.

Laughing at myself I motion my head towards the kitchen. "Come on, I think the tea has gone cold. But nonetheless Ayi and Nia are waiting."

Chapter 22

Staying awake for two weeks was going to be interesting. Especially when you're not quite alone even though there is no one physically here. Yahui found himself wandering the hallway trying to locate the rehearsal room that Lihwa told him about. After she had performed the insomnia spell. She had offered to show him, but he had refused.

Guess I should have asked her to show me after all. Yahui shook his head. Allowing his thoughts to go over the last week. He had no idea how very much his life would change in just a short amount of time. *No. That isn't it at all. His life had always* been destined for this. He had a Fated Soule after all. Fated to be with Lihwa. Just like she was fated to be with him. His hadn't been the first. But he feared as well as knew he would be the last. One way or another, his soule would be the last one in the line of Su Yung's reincarnations.

He heard a distant ring of chimes. With each ringing he felt a wave of affirmation washing over him. *Seems like I am not alone in my thoughts on this matter.* He chuckled aloud. *Not that it would be possible for me to be alone in my thoughts right now anyways.*

Yahui let his hand travel down to the heavy Jade amulet that hung around his neck. The precious stone felt warmer ever since the kiss that Lihwa and he had shared. He wasn't sure why. Perhaps he was just looking for something to be off. And his worried mind was latching on to that. It was more likely that he had just become hotter himself. Why wouldn't the added occupants of his brain not increase the temperature of his body.

Perhaps I should have just stayed in my room. That thought brought him back to the reason he had left in the first place. Not to mention the reason why he hadn't let Lihwa show him the rehearsal room before.

At the time, he thought that just responding to the mountain of texts and emails that he had received while out of commission would be enough to pass the lonely hours of the night. He even answered all the questions from the reporters that sent their questions to his publicist.

Lucky for him his mom had forgiven him for not calling or writing sooner. Mainly because she had left her phone at the office over the holiday, so she wasn't able to get messages to him as well, as he was the last one to write to her prior to that event she was keen to forgive him. That disaster averted he began working on the other overdue tasks. Still he was finished long before the morning light. The emails he thought in hindsight, could have been answered after talking to Lihwa. *Better to ask forgiveness then permission.* Isn't that how that old adage goes? For several of the remaining hours of the night, he had taken to starring at the walls. Wishing that he had brought his laptop with him. At least he could have played the game.

Instead of staying in his room, he was here wandering around trying to find a room in this small town of an estate. Doing his best to stay away from the corridor that would lead him to Lihwa's bedroom door. Ayi had made it clear that Yahui was to remain in the east wing. Ever the protective caretaker. It was interesting to learn that she wasn't just Lihwa's guardian, but her High Priestess to boot.

He had been in numerous costume dramas depicting gods and immortals. He smiled thinking about it. But he never once thought that in his own personal life he would be wrapped up in the most intriguing yet possibly the deadliest drama of them all.

Would this be considered a romance? He found himself wondering before he turned the last corner that Lihwa said would bring him to a pair of sliding doors. She failed to tell him about the magnificent rice paper screens set into the doors that bore beautiful paintings. Knowing just who Lihwa really was, he wouldn't be surprised if these paintings were authentic. The entranceway to the rehearsal room, they should be the doors into a display room.

He laughed out loud when he entered the large room, taken in his surroundings that reminded him of a dojo. Granted the space was perfect for dancing, spacious, and very well padded. There were several matts lining the floor perfect for practicing lifts, and jumps. Not to mention tumbling routines as well. On the two furthest walls there was ceiling to floor mirrors, and a top of the line sound system and stereo stood at the ready in the far corner. Curiosity overtook him when he spied a stack of CDs on a shelf above one of the many speakers. He had only taken three steps into the room before his smile broadened and he ran the rest of the way. His only audience was already inside of his own head, after all. If he wanted to goof off, then he could goof off.

A smile pulled at his lips as he picked up a red pair of pointe shoes nestled on top of a pile of CDs. He caressed the soft silk ribbon between his fingers, rolling them up loosely before placing them on top of one of the large speakers. Curiosity was eating away at him more with each passing second, so much so that he had totally forgotten that he was under a spell. And all the possible negative implications that could entail.

If anyone would have asked him what type of music he thought that Lihwa listened to, Yahui would have guessed c-pop. Never would he have believed the wide array of genres that populated this pile. Everything from classical music from many time periods, Jazz music from the west and even some classic rock and roll. A smile pulled on his lips when he thumbed through the rap music, and alternative rock. She even had a few heavy metal CD's which had some songs that he himself recognized. On the bottom of the pile he found some more electric pop and the aforementioned c-pop. Not to mention a CD case that had his name handwritten in beautiful calligraphy.

Choosing one of her Classic Chinese Folk music CD's, with utmost care he removed the shiny disc from its case before pressing the eject button on the Stereo. Nothing happened. Not a light or a mechanical sound. *It must have a power switch on a surge protector.* He thought as he set the cd down gently on its case, Yahui began his search for the switch.

A long black power strip with five plugins in use rested against the wall behind the stereo systems stand. His finger flicked the switch. A red light emanated from the cord indicating that it was on. He heard the distinct sound of electronics coming to life and then a clicking sound of something moving behind him filling the large spacious room.

Turning quickly Yahui was met by a screen that was lowering from the ceiling and a projector lowering from a hidden panel as well.

The lights dimmed as a picture started to take shape on the screen. Lihwa's lovely face addressed the camera a playfully sweet smile on her lips that met her eyes. The moment that she said his name... he gave her his full attention.

"Xai Yahui, I see you decided to use the rehearsal room after all... I am glad because I wanted you to see this video sooner rather than later. Ayi thinks that I am here practicing for my part in the upcoming TV Drama. So hopefully I can complete this without interruptions.

As you are now aware, I have known your soule for a long time. You made my heart sing when I first met you as Su Yang. You sacrificed your own happiness for that of your beloved brother. The terms of your unhappiness made me always visit you in the dead of night. I would whisper of my love into your ear. And watch a smile bloom on your lips. I had never before found a mortal man alluring. Yet I found Yang to be everything that I wanted in a husband and more.

Su Yang passed away young. Only three years older than you are now. That night I wept my first real tears of heartache. My mother the goddess Lihua came to me with an offer from the Queen Mother Yuanjun. She promised me that your soule would be reborn, Reincarnated, throughout time so that I would always

[164]

be able to love you and watch over you, and so that was what I did.

Over the years I have watched you grow up into a fascinating young man, I have watched you fall in love, marry, and have families. All while I was watching, always watching, over you. You're former self would grow old and die in some reincarnations, and yet in others you would be a warrior and fought in many battles, some that you could not win, and I would be beside you in those times, watching over you, knowing that you would come back to me. Even death couldn't keep me from you.

That is until Wu Xia. I found him, you, sleeping in the forest after bathing in the nearby stream. So handsome, so strong, and so innocent of the world. I entered his dreams and found him pursuing me. Night after night he would call out to me in his dreams and I was all too happy to appear.

Even then I had never been with a man. And yet I would let him dream about caressing me. One night in his dream I sent a fetch. An exact copy of me, into his dream and he pledged his undying love to me with all that he was, every inch of him promised me his heart. And through my fetch I promised.... I promised his soule- your soule- that I would always love him. And that I always have for over six hundred years at that point.

The next day I went to the temple with a few other lesser goddesses. We had been summoned to dance before Longwei. We all gossiped. Even then, there was always gossip. One goddess was saying how she found Wu Xia bathing in the stream and watched him. And how she turned herself into the water so that she would be washing over his skin. I foolishly, I know now, lashed out at her. Telling her that Wu Xia was my love and that she and all others needed to stay away or I would unleash my wrath upon them.

Of course, Longwei heard of this, and after the celebrations where over and after two more nights of laying in Wu Xia's arms in the dreamscape. I was called to Longwei's throne room and condemned for breaking one of his most enforced laws. I had fallen in love with a mortal. The next day I was forced to watch you die." Yahui saw the smoke filled forest and he watched in his mind's eye as Lihwa, no Zhen'ai, called out that she loved him and cried her diamond tears, while a spear impaled him she held him in her arms and wept.

"I died there on that battlefield with you. For you see, Longwei's decree was that you would never be reincarnated again. And my Darling Yahui, you never did in two thousand two hundred and ten years. Until that night in September, the night when you were born. I slept the sleep of the immortals up until that night...

I have watched over you, Yahui, sending my disciples... Ayi and her daughter at first. Out to help watch over you as well. For I feared in my heart that Longwei would awaken and notice just who you were. I stayed away; I went to Academy. I became an educated woman. Learning so much more than ever would have been allowed back before I made myself fall asleep. I learned to speak and read several languages and I even learned how to dance in the way of the humans and create art with my hands instead of with my magic.

I sought out my aunt Meihui and she helped me learn of a way that I could become human. And to stay in the world of the mortals. It was a tricky and difficult spell. A full ritual that Meihui said would leave my human body in a deep sleep for two perhaps three days. I needed to then pray that you would notice me. And that in your own time fall in love with me.

And in your declaration of love would my transformation

into a human be complete. I had visions of your concert and meeting you on that night. The night of the New Year's countdown. Though I knew not anything else. I only knew I needed to be there. I prepared myself and set off to see you. And that dream that I told you was a reality. Well That was the night I started the ritual. It was three weeks later on the 26th, that I awoke and well the rest you know. You might be wondering why am I telling you all this. Well there is a reason my love and the reason is this.

Tonight, you told me you loved me. You declared your love for me, and instead of me becoming complete, I have remained the same. I know not why, only that my transformation is still incomplete. And here is the true reason for my message to you, my darling Yahui.

My fear is that by the end of one hundred and eighty days, (which is now only one hundred and seventy-one days) if I haven't had my transformation completed, I will no longer exist. Not in human form. Nor in my ethereal form, I will fade away and you, my love, will forget me. As you should. For I have caused you so much heartache, pain and yes even death.

I fear that Longwei is right that I am your curse while you have been my greatest gift.

I will end this video with a little dance number." She held up her red point shoes. "One that I performed at my graduation. I know that you would appreciate it as only another dancer could. I love you, Yahui."

Yahui watched the screen with tear filled eyes, holding his fists in his lap. He refused to move until the performance was done. He watched the screen when the music started. It was a song he recognized as coming out in the UK in 2013, five years ago now. Lihwa danced and his eyes were glued to her every move. The music faded out into nothing while he focused on only her movements. The precision of her footwork the angle of her poses. It was just her. And in that moment, he realized the only plausible reason she would make a video like this for him...

"NO, LIHWA!!!" her name tore out of his throat as he ran down the hallway. Racing for Lihwa's bedroom. He had to get there. He just had to see.

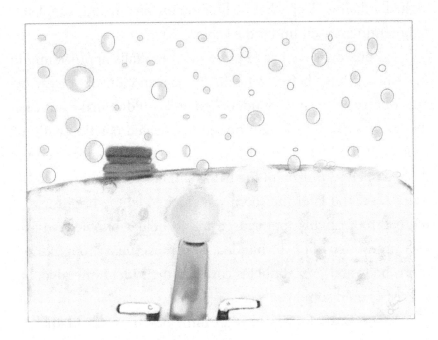

Chapter 23

The relaxing scent of thousands of little Lavender bubbles surrounded me while I reclined in the large in floor bathing pool, the hot water gently swayed back and forth over my skin almost like that of a lover gently caressing me. Yet a lover's touch wasn't what I was in need of. Unless he was going to massage my aches and pains away. I hadn't realized just how sore my body would be after dancing like that... Yet, all my muscles felt tight and sore.

Closing my eyes, I sunk deeper into the warmth of the water, the room was in near total darkness save for the light of the waxing moon pouring in through the skylight. Steam rose all around me, carrying the relaxing aroma into the air. I sighed. inhaling deeply before holding my breath and completely submerging myself under the water.

I heard, as well as felt, the rapid footfalls approaching in the hallway long before I heard the commotion of voices. Ayi and Yahui's voices grew louder. Yet I still couldn't make out what they were saying. I brought myself to a seated position with my head and shoulders above the water. Just seconds before my eyes flashed open in unison of the bathroom door slamming into the wall. A second later the room was flooded by the brightness of the bathroom lights that caused me to hold a bubble clad arm over my eyes so not to be blinded. This movement brought more of my body above the bubbles covering then I had intended, but at least I could somewhat see.

"My Lady, I tried to stop him, but he insisted that he needed to see you immediately," Ayi called over Yahui's shoulder.

Ayi's voice rang through the bathroom echoing off its four walls. Finally, my eyes had adjusted enough to the light to lower my arm. Yahui stood in the doorway gasping for breath. His hungry eyes roamed over the bathing pool lingering on the portions of my body that weren't submerged and hidden by the blanket of bubbles. I could feel my flesh heating up with each second that he continued to stare. Starting with my cheeks and coloring even the tips of my ears with my blushing.

"Did you need something Yahui? Or did you just absolutely need to see me in my bubble bath? I assure you. That if you had indeed rushed here to see me bathe, then now that you've seen me you can turn right around and leave. I am not properly attired for male company." I bit my bottom lip to keep myself from saying anything else. Like how false those words truly were. How much

I wanted him to be with me; yet those thoughts were not proper for a young lady. Especially for one whose caretaker was standing there in the hallway watching over the whole conversation. My face blushed even more when I thought of him joining me, and what Ayi would say at my rash and impure actions.

"Lihwa, I'm sorry!" He turned sharply staying in the doorway, with his back to me he continued, "It's just that I need to talk to you about something that I noticed..." he paused "I realized , or is it remembered... it's all so hard to tell." He placed his palms on either side of the doorframe steadying himself.

"Alright, Ayi, show Yahui to my sitting room and I'll join him there shortly." My voice still quivering from my all to obvious reaction to his nearness.

"As you wish my Lady. Follow me, Mr. Xai, and be happy that I don't have my fan with me, or I would have been happy to have knocked your eyes back into their sockets. My lady is too sweet to scold you but I for one am not!" Ayi motioned for Yahui to walk before her and once he had she closed the door, leaving me once again alone.

I stood wading slowly through the thigh high water to the foot of the stairs. Taking each of the two steps as steadily as I could, my heart was still beating rapidly, and I needed the extra time to calm down. Reaching for the topmost bath towel off of the pile that Ayi had set next to the pool. I wrapped the soft fabric around my torso. The touch of it only made me more aware of the sensations that were coursing through me.

Yet another first for this form, I had to be up in the high thirties by now but to be honest I had lost count. The sudsy water still clung to my skin as I walked across the floor to the wrought iron rack were my red silk bathrobe hung. I attempted to towel off as I went.

Depositing the towel into the hamper I slid the soft silk robe on over my still damp skin. Tying it securely I gazed at my reflection in the tall jade framed mirror that was attached to the wall beside the door. I nearly froze at my reflection. My long hair still dripping down over the smooth fabric, my pale pink eyes smoldering in the light, closing my eyes I breathed in with a large intake of air I exited the room.

Time to see what Yahui needed. And try not to flirt to much in the process.

§

The short walk to the sitting room door normally would have taken me but a few minutes if not just one. Yet when you're having a silent debate with your high priestess on the improperness of my request for her to leave Yahui and myself alone together in the room. Given what I was wearing. The few meters had turn into kilometers in comparison. Finally, albeit grudgingly, Ayi exited the room, but not without looking at me with suspicious yet worried eyes.

I waited for a short count of five before sliding the door open and slowly entering the room...

My sitting room stayed true to the design of the ancient Chinese estates. There were numerous pillows littering the floor. With a line of larger pillows set up around a small table that appeared to hover just centimeters above the teak flooring. Yahui was seated on one of the long pillows he sat with his head in his hands until he heard the door slide shut and looked up to see who had just entered. The emotions that flitted in his eyes were worth a million yuan.

I continued my entrance walking slowly over to him with his eyes never leaving mine. I lowered myself into a kneeling position on a pillow next to him. I watched as he swallowed and parted his lips. Pausing he then reached a shaking hand out to lightly touch a droplet of water that was traveling down my neck on its way towards my breastbone.

His touch was like that of a feather, so soft and gentle. I attempted to stifle a low throaty moan that I could feel welling up inside me. Needless to say, I failed miserably.

"Gods Lihwa, you are a torment... I came to see you because I feared that you had decided to leave. To save me from this curse as you call it. Yet, you walk in as a temptress, a beautiful goddess like you are, wearing that robe with you flesh still glistening from the moisture, and you leave me breathless. I'm not sure how strong you think I am, but I assure you, if I stay here too long, hearing your delicate and sweet moans, I will be no better than my past self in my attempts to take you." He closed his eyes at the same time as closing his hand, he left it there hovering next to my face, making no attempt to move it.

"Lihwa? What is your desire? My heart? It is yours. My soule? Again, I give it to you willingly. My body? All you need do is ask and I will give you that and more. Lihwa, you are my past, my future, and my destiny. I am your fated Soule."

Time slowed; these words were more than I had ever wished to hear. Perhaps I was wrong to be alone with Yahui right now. For I too felt the uncontrollable urge to give myself to him. As an offering, granted it would only be a small gesture compared to the sacrifice and offering that he had just bestowed upon me.

"Yahui, my darling, Xai Yahui. I only desire your happiness. I am here because you live. I breathe the air as you do because somehow you came back to me. I know not why? And I am not foolish enough to have questioned it. But I too fear that I want to give in to your touch. I, Yahui, want it more than I should." I bit my lower lip pausing briefly before continuing. My eyes focusing on his outstretched hand. "Whatever you need to talk to me about please say it now. Before I also give in to my own weaknesses."

The room fell silent, the only sounds that I heard were the thunderous beats of my own heart in my ears. Yahui slowly opened his hand again this time leaning his whole body forward as he reached to touch my face.

"I remember hearing your voice when I was asleep. I remember you telling me to search for you in the darkness. I remember feeling this amazing warmth that lit up the darkness several moments before you woke me up." His hand lingered on my cheek before sliding down to my neck, my wet hair tangling around his fingers.

"Lihwa, you are the most beautiful woman I have ever encountered." He closed his eyes shaking his head briefly before opening them again. "Please forgive my forwardness. It is so hard to fight back these feelings. Least of all fighting back all these thoughts that I might share but would never act on. Not unless."

But what it was that was he was waiting for I didn't need to hear, for I knew that his gallantry wouldn't let him do what I took upon myself to do instead.

Moving faster than a normal human would I let my lips find his. The thunderous tremors that I felt earlier returned and the heat between us grew. Bringing my arms around his neck I drew him closer deepening the kiss. If ever there was a kissing contest to find a kiss that would outshined all the rest this one would surely be a contender. Yahui moaned out as he pulled away smiling, slowly opening his eyes before leaning away.

"I think that we will need to call in the paramedics if they have us do a kissing scene." His hands trembled as he leaned back grasping his head. I will need to invest in some headache medicine as well,

"I'm not so sure if I would be able to stop if I heard them call cut." My own body shaking uncontrollably.

"I think that we should call this a night. I have found my limit, my goddess. If we kiss once more, I will give in to all of the voices that are clamoring in my head. And if we do."

"Yes." *I too needed to manage these feelings.* "I understand, Yahui? Um. I will consider what you have said about the darkness and the light." I stood bowing to him, before realizing that I had just shown him more of myself then I had meant too. My face filled with the heat of embarrassment.

"You really need to stop blushing like that in front of me." He was on his feet quicker than I thought possible for him and he held my face between his warm hands. "I find that color absolutely irresistible." his lips brushed lightly over each of my cheeks before he lightly kissed my forehead.

"I know that we must take my feelings with a pinch of salt right now, but please believe me when I say this. I do have very deep feelings for you Lihwa. Sweet dreams." he released his hold on me and walked to the sliding door without looking back he exited the room, leaving me alone with each nerve ending in my body quivering body firing.

Sighing, I sank back down onto the pillows bringing the one that Yahui had just occupied to my chest. Clutching it tightly to me, I was trembling uncontrollably. Was this what humans feel? Gods how do they stand it? I clutched at the pillow as tight as I could trying to calm my racing heart. For all the good it did, all at once, I felt like my body was ablaze. I closed my eyes and sighed out the name of the man who had just set my soule afire.

"Yahui..."

Chapter 24

The drive to Haku's house in the morning felt like it took forever. Every second that Yahui sat close to me I felt the need to touch him. Yet I battled with myself staring off at the passing landscape through the window.

"I can feel the tension in the air." Yahui burst out laughing. "Are you sure that you want to be alone with me right now? I mean if you need to have Nia…"

"No! No that won't be necessary. We are adults. And not animals. So I think we shall be able to behave ourselves." *At least for another week. Until the full moon- and Meihui's message!* I thought to myself while I plastered a convincing smile to my lips.

"Oh, you are a horrible liar! But you blush so well, that I think this day will be quite interesting!"

I slapped my hand onto his arm, his look of pure shock was enough to make me smile broadly.

"That hurt." He laughed rubbing his arm before he snatched my offending hand and intertwined his fingers with mine. "There, now you can't hit me again. And I will never let you go!"

"Never? Really... that is gonna make me having to use the restroom that much more embarrassing." I laughed full heartedly staring at Yahui while he cringed slightly.

"Yeah, you think that will be embarrassing, just wait until I have to go."

"Oh, no. Whatever will Haku think." I laughed. If he thinks that is going to embarrass me, he has another thing coming...

"Haku? Why would he think anything about it? You really have no idea what he is truly like- and today you will see what a day in the life of a TV drama Star is actually like." He smiled before he brought my hand to his lips. Kissing the back of my hand with a wink he brought our combined hands to the steering wheel turning on the blinker.

"Are we there already?" My cheeks were still rosy from his kiss. But I wasn't ready to face Haku yet. Though I knew that we must. For if we are late Yahui is sure that Haku will make our lives harder than they already are. And they already are hard enough! Oh gods, were they ever.

"This is the next to the last turn we will need to take to get to Haku's house. I am sure that we will encounter the security guard's vehicle escort soon. Honestly, these last few days have been the first in a long time that I haven't had round the clock security. For all the trouble we are in, I have enjoyed the ability to just be me—well—you know what I mean."

The sad thing was that I knew exactly what he meant. Yahui had over a week without an army of security tagging along everywhere he went. I only now noticed the black Jeep Cherokee that pulled out behind us earning a sigh from Yahui.

"And so, it begins, I imagine that the production company will have an agent and an assistant at Haku's for you. It's normal to have these employees, for that is now what they will be to you, the same gender as the entertainer. You being all female." He smiled giving me another sly wink. "You will have two females and I regretfully will have to break a promise to you."

"What?" I pouted

"They won't let me go with you no matter how much I want to keep hold of your hand. The moment that they meet you in the courtyard they will usher you off to get sized and to sign a million pieces of paperwork."

I had totally forgotten about those details. Yet I could see that he was truly sorry to have to be parted from me. He brought my hand up to his mouth sliding his lips over my skin from one side to the other. *Was he sorry to be parted from me or was it just my hand?* I giggled at the thought. Yahui eyed me suspiciously as he turned into a gated drive.

"What is so funny?"

"Oh, well it's nothing really." I shivered slightly from the loss of his lips on my hand. *Perhaps it is I who will miss his lips.* I laughed again. "I was just wondering if you were sorrier to be parted from me or just sorry to be parted from my hand." I giggled again before adding. "Sorry. It was just too funny to not laugh."

"Well of course it was. I mean look who had the thought." his smile was contagious.

"You're awful." I shook my head before adding. "Will we really be separated all day?"

He paused and his face lost his precious smile, a look of resolve took its place. "Not if I can help it!"

Unfortunately, he couldn't help it. As predicted the drive was full of security, a stern faced Haku, and three females that from their attire were most definitely there to fly me away.

Yahui placed the Jeep into park, the look of defeat etched onto his face yet when he turned to me his eyes were apologetic.

"I know that I said that they would be here. But never before in my life had I wished I was wrong so much as I did before pulling into Haku's driveway. We can still leave. I haven't unlocked the doors." He reached his hand to my face stroking my cheek tenderly with his thumb. His eyes searched mine for a long moment before he sighed and shut off the engine.

"I didn't say anything about shutting off the engine. I didn't say anything at all actually." I laughed.

"You didn't have to. It's all written in your eyes."

I flipped down the sun visor and looked at my reflection in the mirror. Yahui's booming laughter exploded from his lips and he reached over flipping the visor back into place.

"Come here my beautiful fool. And let me kiss you goodbye. Cause the moment we get out of the Jeep we won't have time," his hand pulled me closer.

"If you insist." I smiled before meeting his lips with mine, a loud and persistent knocking a few minutes later made us part. It was probable for the best. My body had started quivering again and that wasn't going to make my day any easier. Haku pointed to his watch and then at Yahui before motioning for him to follow him.

A long sigh left my lips and I leaned in kissing his lips briefly one last time before turning my body to the door making ready to open it.

"Wish me luck. Stay safe, my love." I whispered the last part.

"Don't open it. I'm coming around." Yahui said insistently while he opened his door and jumping out, he rounded to my side before the security and the pack of female assistants could gather. Once my door was open, he took my hand and helped me down to the gravel.

"Miss Wu?" a lovely woman, looking to be in her late thirties, called out to me while I took a reluctant step away from the Jeep, away from Yahui. Away to a day spent surrounded by strangers.

"Yes? Please call me Lihwa." The woman flushed and bowed.

A light tugging on my fingers was the last I felt of Yahui's hold before he too was ushered off by Haku. From the way Haku was looking at Yahui, I was kind of glad that I wasn't in his shoes, and that these ladies will have me somewhere far away before the coming explosion. With one last look over my shoulder, I watched Yahui enter the house.

A large white luxury van waited on the other side of the driveway. I walked surrounded by the three ladies and a group of four security guards. The woman who I first thought was in her thirties proved to be nearing fifty.

She asked me to call her Ms. Song, and told me that she is my new manager/ agent. Seeing as I didn't have one already. The other two I found out where my publicist: Lu Meiling, and my stylist: Xi Zhi. Ms. Song was the most vocal of the bunch, and hurriedly told the driver to bring me to the main office of the production company to sign the official paperwork.

§

Three hours later found me sitting in a chair having my hair and make-up done for a photoshoot. Ms. Song said I needed head shots for the company and Meiling well she was asking for a few more to be done so that she could send them around to local advertisers. 'To get my face out to the public.' She said I had to roll my eyes. As if the viral videos (Yahui would be so proud of my use of the proper terminology) from the New Year's concert wasn't public exposure enough. My only reprieve was knowing that Yahui was on his way to join me for those shoots.

"So we will have couple shot done?" I had asked as the stylist was finishing my lipstick.

"Why yes! You are a couple after all. And seeing as Xai Yahui has openly announced your courtship. It is wise to have as many photos done together as we can." Meiling smiled...

"Our courtship?" my voice sounded higher than normal, my surprise evident.

"Oh yes, the emails that he sent with the response to the reporter's questions, he states that he is courting you, and hopes that you will agree to be his wife soon. Had you not read the article? I know that I sent you an email with it attached this morning."

Heat rose up over me, I hadn't read it. Of course to have read it I would have had to check my emails. And I have yet to log on to the address that the company had set up for me on the first. I had already been strongly reprimanded by Ms. Song for my lack of communication. I explained to her that I had left my phone in Yahui's Jeep on the first and had only just found it. Being a human with goddess powers came in handy when I produced my cell phone with a dead battery.

The room became hectic with activity. Security and the workers dashing around, it wasn't until all the young females whispered excitedly, so I could tell who must have made an entrance on site.

Yahui's smiling face emerged moments later to loud giggles and sighs from the staff and stylists. All who watched him with expectant eyes the moment that he walked my way. His brown eyes gleamed while he walked around weaving through the amassing workers. He stopped only once, and that was to talk to Meiling for a moment before he nodded and met my eyes once more.

"You miss me, my goddess?" Yahui smiled his ears red from his slip of the tongue. "I know I missed you!" He bent and placed a warm kiss on my cheek. Before whispering. "Sorry about that. We'll have to work on pet names for each other."

I laughed shaking my head. "You are so cute when you are flustered, Gorgeous. I did miss you. You have no idea how much..." Yahui wrapped his arms around my waist and pulled me to him. My body fit snugly against his.

"Oh, well then we better enjoy this photo shoot because we will be apart for the next few days." His voice was like velvet, but in my head warning bells and whistles were going off.

"You think that is wise?" I whispered into his ear hugging him back tightly.

"I refuse to live in fear, and besides we will be surrounded by people the entire time- and as I won't be sleeping- we can play our computer game and I can work out during your downtime." He laughed and with a light kiss to my forehead we parted.

Every step that he took away from me felt like a hundred kilometers, but I understand what he was saying- no matter how much I hated it.

Yahui pulled me towards the set that was made up for the shoot and I made a silent request for Ayi to place wards on both Yahui's house and Haku's if we were going to be apart- I wasn't going to leave him without some form of protection. Upon Ayi's affirmative response I smiled relaxing into Yahui's arms for the beginning of what was to be a long photo shoot.

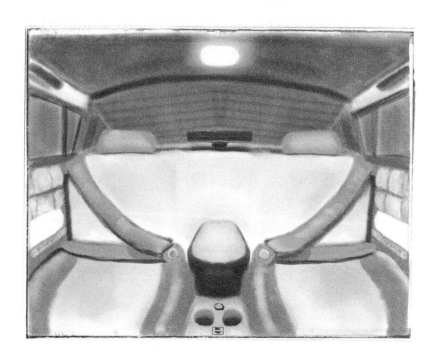

Chapter 25

It was nearing ten pm when I was ushered, albeit reluctantly, to an awaiting black SUV. Yahui was able to keep his promise and spent as much time together with me as possible. Yet, even that wasn't enough time for me.

"Have a goodnight's sleep." He whispered into my ear bringing my body closer to his in a warm comforting embrace. "I'll be on the game later, say around midnight, that way we can meet up there. If you are still awake. Don't stay up for me if you are tired." His lips brushed mine with a light kiss before lifting me up and placing me gently down on the rear seat. Stepping closer he captured my lips once again giving me yet another brief kiss. No matter how brief the kiss was the intensity of it sent shivers up and down my spine. Yahui stepped back and with a sigh, that I'm not sure was his or mine, he closed the door.

I stared out the window all the while that we drove away... not looking away from his fading form until we had turned left out of the parking lot, and we were heading towards my estate.

"It's never easy for you to say goodbye, is it?" A warm familiar voice forced me to turn around and look beside me.

"Meihui! You are so early- I wasn't expecting to see you until the full moon." my voice had risen an octave higher than normal and I tried to steady my tone as I continued. "It's always an honor, Meihui." I leaned in kissing her cheek in greeting. A broad warm smile graced her face, wiping away the look of shock that was there a moment ago from my shrill greeting.

"The honor is mine, sweet girl. Truthfully, I didn't expect to see you both out of the estate. When the Queen told me that you weren't there, I decided that you needed to know sooner rather than later, the details of how to get Yahui back to himself. Although, after seeing you both together I am hesitant to even say." Her sly smile wavered, and her lips trembled for the briefest of moments before she clasped my hand into hers. I felt a wave of power wash over me. The intensity of it was enough to have made any normal human women jump back in alarm. But I did not move.

Meihui's eyes softened as she looked down at our joined hands. "I was wrong, my dear sweet Zhen'ai, I was a fool to advise you against allowing the past lives to reconcile their love for you."

"What? But won't that...?" I gasped. *She had been adamant before that I shouldn't allow the past lives to reconcile their love for me. Or I would be lost to Yahui forever. She even gave me the amulet*

[185]

for Yahui to wear. Were these things in vain? As if she had read my thoughts as openly as though I had said the words aloud, she gave answer to them.

"I don't know; it's a possibility. Oh Zhen'ai, it is a risk that you'll have to take. If you intend to correct the wrong that Longwei has done. Then you must allow each of the past lives to surface. The Queen says that once each has, well... once each has fulfilled their deepest truest desire. Then and only then will they return to their rest- leaving Yahui's body."

My hands trembled, and Meihui, squeezed them before she continued. Raising her gaze up to look me in the eyes.

"Dearest Niece, I know that this will be a torment."

"No, no it's not a torment, it's just like Longwei to figure out a way to drive me away from the man I love. He is sure that I wouldn't be willing to give up my life for Yahui's. Well, it looks like I will once again have the honor to prove to Longwei the one thing he never gives credence too," a smirk crossed my lips...

Meihui's eyes grew wide. "Oh, and what is that?" Her eyes searching mine for the answer. Yet finding none.

"That he is wrong, it's the one thing he never thinks he can be." The coldness in my voice even made me shiver. Yet I knew my words to be true.

We spent the remainder of the ride to the estate talking about what I needed to do- and just how to do it. Then Meihui left the same way she appeared. Without detection from the two security guards that occupied the front seats.

My mind raced over the information that had just been revealed to me. And try as I might, I couldn't figure out the best way to explain what needed to be done to Ayi.

It's funny really, out of Yahui and Ayi, it was her that I was unsure how to tell.

Yahui would be easy. I would explain it all in full detail. But Ayi, if she knew that there was even a whisper of a chance that I might not survive in the end. Well, she wouldn't understand. Not that Yahui will. But when it is just a question of telling him, it would be more troublesome trying to figure out a way to tell Ayi, then it would him. In all honesty, I was more worried about how he was going to react when I told him that there was a huge possibility that one of his past lives would have to do some acting. I shivered at the thought.

When the SUV came to a stop, I knew what I had to do. Thinking a silent prayer, I opened the door and took my first real step towards the future. A future where I had to surrender to the past to ensure that the man that I love lives his life...

Regardless of if I'm in it or not.

Starting tonight—everything is going to change.

§

The bedroom was silent an hour later. I sat on my bed with the laptop in my lap waiting for the appointed hour so that I could connect to Yahui. I needed to ensure that the spell I wove while sitting here would work.

Normally it needed two high priestesses to work the spell properly (Seeing as I was human now, I was basing all my spell casting on the fact of my mortality). But I hadn't found the nerve to tell Ayi yet. I had said a few silent prayers that I would not have too. If this spell does work, then this will be how we manage to get through the future filming process. If not, I will have to break down and tell Ayi that I need her help, which, of course, will lead to her wanting to know what is going on. All of it. She would not be satisfied with only learning of bits and pieces.

The dinging of the notification bell let me know that Yahui

had logged on to the game, a full nine minutes early. A message box opened and the connection to Yahui was locked. Normally this is when I would begin to speak to him. Feeling the vibrations of his voice in my ear. But that wasn't how this evenings gaming was going to be done. Nor any other time going forward for the unforeseeable future. Or until my time is up and I fade away...

I felt the power of the spell tingling through me. With one last look at the door to check that I had indeed locked it, I closed my eyes and whispered the words that will bring me to him. His full name....

"Xai Yahui"

∫

There was an odd sound of water trickling over stones, and a gentle breeze that blew my hair around me tickling my nose in the process. I kept my eyes closed until I heard the all too familiar voice of Yahui render all the other noises and sensations irrelevant. My eyes flew open to find Yahui's avatar standing before me. His warriors armor gleaming in the glow of the digital sunshine. The red and silver seemed to be even more brilliant than it did when I viewed it on the computer screen.

"Lihwa, this is incredible, I probably should be freaking out but I must admit that this is so above what I was expecting when I told you I would meet up with you online..."

He strode across the landscape coming to a stop before me. A playful smile pulled at my lips as my eyes searched his. Even computer generated he was absolutely gorgeous. I took a moment to look at my hard-earned mandarin outfit that we had worked so long to get all those nights ago. It was so soft, and the silk poured over my body like the water in the stream that we stood next to.

"Oh gods, I am so glad that this worked." I sighed, resting

my hand on my sword. "In all honesty, I wasn't sure I'd be able to pull this off on my own. But I see that I haven't lost my ability to cast." I walked over to the small footbridge. Yahui smiled briefly, following closely.

The view was like something from the ethereal world. The grass had a distinct purple hue to its normal green tones. And the water was such a beautiful crystal blue. Like no earthly water I had ever seen. A knowing glint passed over my eyes. It had to be one of the former gods who designed this world. It was no wonder that humans loved to travel here. It was most likely bewitched.

"Ahem."

The sound of Yahui clearing his throat brought me back to myself. I turned slowly, deliberately, straight into the waiting arms of the man that I love... His lips covered mine, as I felt the longing in his kiss. His tongue met mine twinning in a dance of their own. I found myself pressed between his body and the railing of the bridge.

My arms wrapped around his neck pulling him closer, deepening the kiss further, before gasping for breath. We parted gazing at each other in a way that I had never seen him do before, not in this lifetime nor in any other.

"Wow," I panted. "That was unexpected. Welcome, oh so very welcome. Unexpected but welcome." I laughed, resting my forehead on his chest.

"I'm sorry. I know that was extremely forward of me, but I've been wanting to do that since New Year's, and this, well, this is the first time that I've been alone with you."

"Not really, we've been alone a few times since then.... And if you have forgotten the kisses that we have shared?"

"No, I mean alone." He pointed to his head. "In here, in

this game, it's just me. No other stow away occupants. Just you and me. How did you do it?" His eyes searched mine while his hand stroked through my hair. The feeling of his caresses sent bolts of electricity through me. "Have you figured a way to break the curse?"

When I was in the SUV after Meihui's revelation, I believed that I had the perfect way to tell Yahui how we were going to correct this horrible misdeed. However, I shook my head slightly. How do I tell him that to free him, I need to imprison him in the realm of a computer game? Especially after that kiss? The type of kiss that I so desperately long for. I gazed deeply into his brown eyes choosing my next words carefully.

"I haven't fixed it yet, but I know what we have to do."

"Really?" He sighed, pulling me into a tight bear hug. "By the gods, that is wonderful news." He laughed, and for the first time in days, it was his amazing carefree laugh of his that I loved so very much. "What do we need to do? I will do anything to be able to free myself and you so that we can be together forever. Believe me Lihwa, I love you!" He pushed me back against the railing again looking me in the eyes. "Do you hear me?"

His eyes searched mine... Looking for some sign that this had been what my human body needed. His declaration of love. But... It wasn't going to work. Not here, not in this realm that only existed because I made it so...

"Yahui, my beloved, while it is true that I believe your words, and know that you speak of your own heart... Your words, while they warm my very soule and give me such joy. Haven't made my transformation in real life complete... But I will not lose heart, so don't you dare either." I took in a deep breath encouraged by the resolute look in his eyes I continued. "Meihui, told me how to break the curse. But to do so you will need to go to sleep. And we will need to release the past lives one at a time." His smile washed away with those words.

"You will have to be with them you mean?" I saw the hurt in his eyes. "You'll have to share yourself with each of my past lives before we can be together?" His tone was flat, lifeless. It was the first time that I actually believed that we were in fact in a computer game.

I bit my lip, pausing for a heartbeat before giving my response. "I don't know what they will require of me in order to be released. But—" I couldn't say the words. Not when his eyes looked so hurt and were staring right at me. So instead of words I nodded my response. A piece of me cringed waiting for him to yell. But he didn't, as a matter of fact, he was the absolute opposite. He was deathly silent.

He stayed that way looking off into the distance his hands still holding my arms. We had to have stayed that way for an hour, maybe more, I wasn't sure, but it was too long, and I was scared. I needed him to tell me what he was thinking.

"Yahui, my love. Please, say something. Anything." My voice was so different, there was a tone of desperation that I had never heard, not even when I was begging Longwei to spare Xia's life all those years ago. "If you don't want to, we—"

"We? We what, Lihwa? We let you die, and I never remember you? I go on living as a freak with all these voices, yet I don't know why they are there? No, that isn't acceptable. We will do this. We will let loose my past selves on the present. But tell me," —his eyes met mine again, looking like the eyes of someone facing defeat. so tired and desperate— "Why did you construct this?" His hand released my arm while he made a sweeping motion all around us. "Is this where we will be able to be together, only here until this nightmare is over? Do we have to start now? Do we have time to do the filming in a few months, heck, do we have time to do the filming tomorrow?"

"Yes, I constructed this for your soule to connect to. It is no surprise that it is only the two of us in here. I cast the spell so that it would be such. No, we don't have to start tonight, but we must start soon. I only have a set number of days before I revert into nothingness. And while I can recall all twenty of your past lives I am unsure just how many reside inside your human mind."

He blew out a deep breath. "Give me a chance to step down from filming."

"I don't think we will have to. I think that seeing as this is a period piece and your character is supposed to be a warrior that this will be perfect. You know, even though the you that is here and now is a performer, the you from the past, aren't that much different." I paused briefly before adding. "Just maybe a little more forceful."

"You are saying that you think my past lives can do this role?"

I nodded, "And if there are any problems I will bring them here to rehearse and learn from your mastery. We don't have to worry about that right away. We have two months."

He chuckled, a dry mirthful sound, and then he sighed. "Looks like you've done a lot of planning in the short time that we were apart. Can I at least have one more day. And then we will remove the spells and we shall deal with this monumental case of multiple personalities." Again, I nodded. I started to step away from him when I was suddenly pulled back into his embrace.

His lips were more demanding than ever as they assaulted my own. He pulled away only briefly before he scooped me up into his arms. Striding three steps before leaping into the air.

We flew for several meters, the colorful landscape beneath us blurring past before coming to rest in front of a cottage.

His smile broadened. "I spotted this cottage off in the distance a little while ago. If I'm going to be sharing you with the likes of Xia in a matter of days, then I will have my way with you first." His eyes narrowed wickedly. "After we wed of course."

I looked up and noticed that there was a small chapel beside the cottage, it was the in-game equivalent of a wedding hall. I bounced in his arms with each step that he took. Wrapping my arms around his neck.

When I spoke, my words came out in a low, throaty purr. "As you wish."

Chapter 26

Yahui, you want steamed buns for breakfast? I'm putting in the order now, so when we get to the studio in the morning it will be ready for us." Haku's voice rang through the room, bringing Yahui out of the most intense daydream he had ever had. Or was it? His eyes flitted to the clock and watched as the time changed to 23:52 hours.

"Yahui? Did you hear me man?" Haku entered the office shaking his head when he noticed that Yahui was staring at the login screen. "You told her that you'd be on at midnight. Don't get yourself all worked up if she isn't there yet."

A sly smile played at Yahui's lips as he remembered the

events that just transpired. Hours in game happening in only a minute of real-world time. Being in love with a Goddess had some serious benefits.

"Yeah, steamed buns sound great. Now see yourself out; I want alone time."

"Geez you're touchy tonight. If this is about what I said earlier, I'm sorry/not sorry. You've only known her for a week for god's sake and you're already talking 'white stone houses and two point five kids.' Whatever man. I'm outta here. Just make sure you're up and ready to go by 0700."

Giving Haku a brief salute, Yahui turned his attention back to the screen. A message notification flashed across his screen.

"It worked. Lol"

He smiled placing his hands on the keyboard he hurriedly typed his response.

"I would say so. Best gaming ever."

"I bet you say that to all your in-game wives."

"All of them? How many in game wives do you think I've had?"

"A few—at least more than one."

"Your words wound me, Madame, I'll have you know that you are my first. As I have never taken an in-game wife, well, other than in a drama—but that doesn't count."

"If you say so. ;P"

Yahui laughed leaning back into his chair.

His eyes watched the three little dots that told him Lihwa was typing. When her response appeared he was saddened but not surprised. After all they had been through a full eight-hour night even if it had only been one minute here.

"I'm exhausted, and if I'm gonna be any good in the morning, I'll need to turn in. I wish I was back laying in your arms. Even if we had those weird censorship rectangles to deal with."

"The sexiest rectangles I have ever seen," he typed before he laughed looking again at the three dots that flashed. He missed having his headset. But he had been happy that Haku let him use one of his gaming laptops. It was an older model, but it worked just as well.

"Yes you wore yours exceedingly well. Goodnight my love. I'll see you in the morning at the studio."

His fingers tapped on each key with a longing that he had never experienced before in his life.

"I wish I was able to hold you in my arms as well. Asleep or not., just to watch you slumber in my arms would be worth the passing hours. But good night my wife. We are having steamed buns for breakfast. Remember to bring your appetite."

Yahui spent the next hour in-game, gathering resources (food, health, weapons, manna), he hoped would transfer into substances that he could live off while he spent these upcoming days living in the game. When Lihwa first mentioned the idea of possibly bringing his past lives here to rehearse for the part, he had thought her insane. There weren't enough hours to adequately teach a novice how to act. Yet, knowing that they were able to spend eight hours to every minute here the impossible became possible. The downside was that he was going to have more than enough time spent by himself. Perhaps he will teach himself a new skill. Or language. At least he would be able to sleep, that would help pass the time.

Steam filled the bathroom several hours later. It was nearing 0600 and he wanted to be showered and ready for when it was time to leave. Lihwa had already texted him, and from the words she didn't say (which was a lot seeing as she sounded so formal and not her normal self). He knew that he was going to tell Haku exactly what he could do with his insistence that he stay at either Haku's place or his own home during these first few weeks of filming.

If he was going to be cast aside while his body was used to enjoy the pleasures of Lihwa's touch, then he was going to stay with her at least one night before any other past life claimed her.

She occupied his thoughts constantly (a hazard of not sleeping) and even now as he shaved and styled his hair, he wondered what she was doing at that very moment.

His mind wandered to the memory of her sauntering into the sitting room wearing that thin red silk robe. And the way that her body was hugged by the flowing fabric, and the glistening of her still wet skin and how she moaned so delicately when he trailed his finger over her skin. Even in game she had sounded just the same, albeit censored.

Knocking on the door jolted him to the present.

"Yahui?" More knocking. "You alive in there? You know that is my shower too, right?" Haku's voice sounded through the door. It was a good thing that he was done shaving prior to the deafening knocking, or he would have had a true scar for his character.

Opening the door, Yahui threw a towel at Haku's face before with a smirk he walked down the hallway back to the guest bedroom.

∫

The ride to the studio seemed to take forever. Every bump in the road Yahui swore that Haku was swerving just to hit them. Causing Yahui's fingers to slip over the wrong icons on his cell phone. He had already sent three unreadable text messages to Lihwa, before he sighed out in exasperation and placed his phone back into his pocket.

"Are you done torturing me yet? Or am I still being punished for the two days that I didn't respond to your beck and call?"

If it was anyone other than Haku, Yahui wouldn't have said a thing, but a pink slip would have found a way into their possession before the end of the day.

"I'm still salty that you have totally broken the bro code. I never would have brought you to that shopping district had I known that you were gonna ditch me like this."

"Ditch you? Man- you're the one who ninety-five percent of the time is off mooning over some girl or another. And I have to rely on my other assistance to get a hold of you. At least now that I have Lihwa, you'll never have to worry about where I am. Because, I'll be with her!"

"Whatever man. Just keep your valuables stashed. No need to lose the family jewels to someone who is digging for them."

That was the straw that broke the proverbial camel's back. "You think that she is with me because I am famous, and for my money? You have no idea how wrong you are. Honestly, tonight after the shoot, you are going to Chauffeur me over to her home. And then we shall discuss just how wrong you are- it's not only me that you will need to apologize to."

"Ok, and if you find out that I am right then you will need to chauffeur me around for two weeks. And grovel at my feet in apology. I mean hands and knees groveling- none of that electronic stuff..."

Yahui laughed internally, "You're so on. But if those are your stakes then mine will have to be that you won't interfere with me staying at Lihwa's home... For as many days and or nights as I want..."

"Agreed"

∫

The remainder of the ride to the studio went by smoothly and without another word being said. The gate to the studio was surrounded by screaming fans. A tightening in the pit of his stomach had him looking around the studio parking lot, looking for the all too familiar black SUV that he had first seen Lihwa in. When his eyes found it, he let out the breath that he had been holding.

While he had experienced this aspect of stardom several times, this was truly the first time that Lihwa had, and that made him feel extremely anxious. The tightness in his gut didn't subside until a few minutes later when he saw Lihwa striding towards him, a plate of stuffed steamed buns and a bowl of rice porridge in her hands.

"You're late, husband." Lihwa's voice was barely above a whisper yet the wink she added made his worries melt away. Yahui felt a smile form on his lips and he had lowered his mouth to hers without even thinking about the crowd of onlookers that stood around them.

"Um, sorry." Yahui's eyes flashed open only to see the adorable flush of Lihwa's cheeks. "Thank you for breakfast."

"You're very welcome. Thank you. I found the new dressing rooms they have us across the hall from each other. Ms. Song says that is unusual but seeing as how we are a couple, they are trying to accommodate us."

"Ahem!" the unmistakable sound of Haku had Yahui clenching and unclenching his fist before he reluctantly turned to stare at his annoying best friend. *He is my friend.* Yahui had to keep telling himself.

"What is it Haku?" Yahui's voice was flat and almost cold even to his own ears.

"The new scripts have just arrived for today's shoot. You may want to have a look at what the writers have added to this lovely test scene."

Passing Yahui a stack of papers bound together with a plastic clip. Haku had it opened to a page that was only a few sheets from the start.

It was almost too good to be true. Yahui's smile broadened with every line that he read.

"And they want us to film this today? Interesting..." Taking the plate of stuffed buns from Lihwa's hand he passed her the papers for her to read.

Yahui sank his teeth into the warm dough while watching the realization and the emotions play on Lihwa's face. Her wide eyes glared at him before softening and a sly smile curved her lips.

"Did you have anything to do with this last-minute change?" She asked snatching the remainder of the steamed bun from Yahui's hand before placing it into her own mouth.

"I did no such thing, but I admit that I will not begrudge them for their creativity. I look forward to seeing you fully dressed in your new wardrobe..." a glint of mischief flashed in his eyes. With the last stuffed steamed bun on the plate Yahui smiled before turning to walk to his dressing room, Haku in tow.

Chapter 27

L ihwa, Ms. Wu? The director is requesting that you come out in full costume so that they can determine if they need to change the filters on the cameras." Ms. Song peeked her head into the door, not even bothering to knock before doing so.

I ascended from my chair with all the grace that I could muster, and after taking one last long look at my reflection I turned and strolled out the door into the hallway. Ms. Song's frantic footfalls could be heard stampeding down the hallway, she scurried into my dressing room and a few minutes later she returned humbly attempting to pass me a fluffy bathrobe, which I apologetically refused. Holding my head high I walked into the bustling sound stage wearing my costume and a regal smile.

Heads turned and many whispered while I passed them by, but I cared not what they said. I continued towards my intended destination: Yahui.

He was sitting on a chair reading his script fully dressed in his red Silk kimono with the intricate black scrolling design work. The long dark brown hair and top knot made my breath hitch, I hesitated briefly in my purposeful, yet elegant march. Seeing him like this had transported me back to a much different time. Back to a fire lit chambers and a rice paper scroll giving orders to go into battle.

His eyes slowly glanced over the top of the paper. I felt them moving over the curves of my form. A sly smile played at his lips, yet a glint of something far greater flashed in his eyes.

My body was covered, yes it most certainly was, although to say that it was modestly dressed would be a falsehood. The fine ivory silk clung to my body and a fine lace panel bridged the distance from one rounded breast to the other, dropping to a pointed "V" just below my navel. Leaving very little to the imagination. Shimmering golden threads mapped out a beautiful design. Telling the story of the rise of the fabled goddess Zhi Nu up into the stars.

The irony of the depiction had not been lost on me. When I first laid eyes on the fine stitching I nearly cried. For her tale would at least have her remembered. While mine, if all ends in failure, will end with me being forgotten.

Yahui stood and slapped the script into Haku's chest, accomplishing two things. Firstly, it freed up his hands, and secondly it made Haku close his gaping mouth.

"You look incredible! A goddess," his voice dropped into a whisper before he leaned down to place his mouth next to my ear. His whispered words sent a faint shiver over my body. Each syllable casting a gentle breeze over the nape of my neck. "Just like the Goddess that you are, Zhen'ai." I felt his lip's tender caress for the briefest of moments before the chattering of the crowd intensifying around us brought me back to the present. He had just called me Zhen'ai, and my body felt like it was being pulled to him. I shook my head trying to clear it of the thoughts that were beginning to form. I knew that my senses were heightened to a level that wasn't condoned in public, and from the look in Yahui's eyes his were as well.

"You two look incredible together. Places everyone. We will do a brief run through and see if we need to correct the lighting and/or filters on the cameras. Chang, the designs are flawless. Absolutely perfect." The bespectacled man sitting in his director's chair looked over to a red-faced gentleman who was desperately looking through his sketchbook. Chang closed his book at once bowing towards the director before he turned his attention towards me.

I began to suspect that this costume was one that had been designed by someone other than Chang. The who I had yet to figure out. Too many names come to mind, and not enough evidence to prove who the culprit is just yet.

Although, I had my suspicions.

We moved over to our set, a romantic bed chamber... Decorated in many different shades of red. Flowing silks and hand-woven lace work hung from the ceiling, soft pillows lay scattered over a hand stuffed mattress. It was a room fit for an Emperor, or in this case a Goddess.

I lowered myself into a reclining position that had been marked out for me, leaning my cheek onto my hand while the other hand played with a tuft of hair that was the same shade as the ones in Yahui's hairpiece. Yahui laid with his head in my lap feigning sleep. The scene was set, and the director nodded to an assistant with a clapperboard and the first take began...

§

As luck would have it we managed to film the test scene in three takes. I was ushered back to my changing room, wearing the robe (Ms. Song insisted), and changed back into my *street clothes* as she called them.

Yahui said that he would be coming to the estate tonight and I notified Ayi to have cook prepare a feast. For I knew that if Yahui was coming it would not be alone. At least not at first. We had much to do. And very little time to do it. In less than twenty-four hours I would be faced with one of the many past lives that had taken up residence in Yahui's body, *Thank you so much Longwei.*

Tonight, well tonight was going to be the night that I would get to hold onto the man I love... While I prayed that we will once again return to each other and not have this end with me fading away. I knew that we needed to take each moment together as a blessing.

Chapter 28

My Lady, Xai Yahui and a guest has arrived. They are waiting for you in the reception area." Nia's voice called through the door to my chamber. I had thought that I would be able to change at least before they would arrive. Yahui told me that Haku wanted to stop to pick up a few things before coming, and that he had to stop at his house as well... Whatever they were stopping to get couldn't have been that hard to obtain, seeing as they had made it here in record time.

"Thank you, Nia, tell them to make themselves comfortable

and see if the cook is ready for supper. Perhaps you can offer her a hand." At that Ayi laughed

"He will offer her a hand, all right... in eating the food. I assure you that boy has a bottomless pit of a stomach. I don't know where he puts it all. It has to be a paternal trait. He sure didn't get it from our side of the family." Pulling the comb through my long hair and with the nimblest of fingers Ayi began plaiting it. She had my hair up into a beautiful arrangement before I even realized that she was done.

"Thank you, Ayi." Her eyes beamed in her reflection.

"Is everything going well, my Lady... You seem really happy this evening. And young master Xai is here. I can only guess that we will be making plans for a monumental wedding celebration soon."

I smiled through my internal worry. *One moment at a time* I reminded myself.

"Ayi, there will be many hurdles still, but things are looking well, and I am extremely happy this evening." Her gentle hand came to rest on my shoulder and she squeezed me for a split second before bringing her chin down to rest on the spot.

"Then let's not keep the master waiting." She smiled, her lovely smile crinkling the corner of her eyes and added. "You look exquisite like always. He is a lucky man." she beamed.

Ayi liked seeing me happy... Why not show her just how happy I am. With one last inspection I glided out of the chair and skipped to the doorway. Haku was here, and I was intrigued to find out exactly what had made Yahui decide to bring him.

∫

Voices echoed down the hallway to greet me once I rounded the corner. I recognized Yahui's at once, with his smooth melodic tones. Haku's voice, on the other hand, was more of an eclectic array of sounds. His words became clearer once I was within earshot of the room.

"...Yes, you win, she is richer than you. This house is..."

"Estate" Yahui corrected

"Estate, mansion, a small village... Whatever you want to call it. It is amazing. We could do a photo-shoot here once a month and have enough backdrops to keep us busy for a few years. Why have I never heard of her until now?"

I walked into the room allowing myself to lean on the door frame before answering Haku's question.

"I imagine the reason you never heard of me before was because I was residing abroad." Both Yahui and Haku's eyes darted towards me. "I purchased this estate a few years ago and it was a mess. No one had lived here in a long time, so I had to have repairs done. Extensive repairs at that. I only moved in recently. Like I told Yahui the day you both saw me at the shopping district was my first time venturing into town." I looked at my fingers as I began to tick off other reasons. "I went to Academy in Paris where I graduated at the top of my class. I danced in a ballet troupe for a few tours. If you are interested, I can play you a few videos. The quality is fantastic. Do I need to continue?"

Haku's eyes fell to the floor not able to look up at me. "No, Lihwa, that will not be necessary. Please forgive my ignorance."

"You need to apologize for more than that, remember?" Yahui's voice was demanding at once I wondered what had happened to make it so.

"Lihwa, I am an insensitive *mutt* who has formed false opinions of you based on the fact that my friend is spending more time with you than he is with me."

"And..." Yahui waved his hand in the air in a circular motion in front of himself.

"And...?" Haku glared at him, his words coming through his gritted teeth. "You aren't a money hungry jewel digging hussy."

"Hussy? Well that is a new one." Yahui frowned. "When did you say that she was that?"

"I may or may not have said that to the production crew today while you both were in makeup." Haku stood and bowed deeply. "I apologize to the both of you."

"I don't know. These are grave accusations. Is it my understanding that you thought I was only after Yahui because he was famous?"

Haku nodded yet refused to straighten.

"I see. So if you had come here tonight, and I lived in a little shack with barely any money to my name, what? Yahui, what would have had to do exactly?"

"I would have—" Yahui started but when my eyes flashed to him he stopped, raising his hands up in defeat. "Man you're on your own..."

"Um, well. He would have had to chauffeur me around for two weeks and grovel on his." Haku mumbled the last few words they came out a jumbled mess. Yet I understood where he was going with them regardless.

"Hmmm... I see... Why aren't you groveling then? Haku? Was that not the deal? Weren't you to do the same?"

Haku stood rim rod straight. "No, Lihwa, that was not the deal, I was to leave Yahui alone, apologize to the both of you and —uh—let him stay here as many nights as he wanted."

Laughter rolled over my lips, the effect made Haku look at Yahui questioningly...

Yahui only shrugged his shoulders in response.

"Ah. Sorry. I just find this whole situation... odd. I guess my lack of relationship experience makes that so. Haku, you are forgiven." Haku's eyes lit up with relief. "Yet, I fear I have a confession to make, and you might not like it at all. You see," I stepped into the room, walking over to where Yahui sat, running my fingers through his soft brown hair until my hand stroked lightly down his cheek. "I plan on occupying all of Yahui's free time over the next few months. I fear that I will be the cause of a separation between the two of you, And to that end I will admit, I am... not at all... sorry."

Haku laughed. "When this day started I would have never bet it would end this way. But I concede. Who am I to stand in the way of love. Especially a love that can make Yahui speechless. Now that that is over. Can we all eat? The food smells delicious."

Yahui stood folding me into his arms. His brown eyes stared deeply into my own. I'm not sure how long we stood there before he spoke, it could have been seconds or minutes for all I knew, but the moment he spoke his words brought me from the trance that he had me under.

"Yes Haku, I think that it is safe to say it's time to eat."

∫

The food was spectacular, as always. Except the urgency that was in Yahui's eyes made me wish that the number of courses was limited to just two. Instead of the four that cook had prepared. When we finally were able to guide Haku out of the house. The building intensity between Yahui and I was felt by everyone around us. Ayi dragged Nia out of the main house towards the guest cottage under the pretense that there was work that needed to be done there.

It wasn't even two seconds after they were out the door before Yahui rushed over to me scooping me up in his arms like he had in the game.

"Are you wanting to fly me to the moon, my love?" My throaty question came out like a purr rather than my voice.

"No," he said, walking slowly, me cradled to his chest. "No, I just want to hold you in my arms from now until it is time for me to sleep. I need you, Lih—" He stopped, a quizzical look on his face.

"What is it my love?" I asked.

"You know, I just thought of something. Why? Why did you change your name? It had certainly been enough years since you were a household deity that your true name isn't as widely known. So why call yourself Wu Lihwa when your given name is so beautiful." His eyes searched mine as his lips parted emitting his hypnotic whisper. "Zhen'ai..."

"Names have power, Yahui. That's why... For example, a god (or a goddess for that matter) need only say my name to summon me." My lips pressed together into a thin line before I sighed heavily then added. "You seem to have that hold over me as well. Every time you say my true name I feel a distinct tugging of my being to you. But to answer your question. I asked Ayi to put her head together with Nia to come up with an alternate name, because I didn't want to be having a conversation with a normal human and all of a sudden disappear from in front of them.. I don't think that they would understand."

"Ah, I see. If I was, say, in my bedroom alone, and I called out your true name, you would have to come to me?" A mischievous smile spread wide over his face, making me wish I hadn't mentioned the fact that he had that effect on me too. "This is very interesting information. Does this happen with everyone when they say your name?"

I had to stop and think. My eyes fixed on the carved wooden beam that hung above our heads. Looking at the way the lines were so delicate and true. I followed them as they carved out a scene of a waterfall and a lotus flower before I responded.

"Huh, no... The answer is no, not everyone. Usually it will draw my attention. Much like when my faithful followers would pray to me, I would instantly hear the prayer. But I wasn't summoned completely to them. But you're different. You draw me to you like how an ethereal being would. How strange." I let my eyes roam over his face, searching for any signs that he was in fact not truly human. But I knew that he was. I had witnessed his birth. Although it was only by chance that I had. I woke up to a prayer and felt his soule's presence while he was still in his mother's womb. It was a miracle.

Yahui let out a soft chuckle. "What are you thinking that has your brow all wrinkled up like that?"

I tried to smile while I looked up into his eyes. I couldn't come right out and say. I was wondering if you are not human... So I came up with the next best truth. "I was just thinking about how very blessed I am to have you here, Yahui. You are truly a gift. A precious gift that brought me from darkness into the light."

He halted at the door to my bedroom. "I feel the same way about you. I have been given the greatest gift of love, so pure and true. Even with all that has happened. I don't want to waste a single second that has been given to us. This doesn't happen every day. I know that. That is why I am here tonight. That is why I am willing to stay locked up in a video game for gods know how long," He smiled, shaking his head. "Did you know that for every minute here it is eight hours there?"

Shifting me in his arms Yahui grabbed the doorknob and attempted to open the door. His face gave away nothing, but I knew he was having a hard time. I, myself, have a hard time with this door and that is when I'm carrying nothing. *A little covert help won't hurt.* I thought, so on his next try I blew out a little breath of air and the door opened wide.

He smiled at his accomplishment, and I stifled a giggle by burying my face into his neck.

"Your bedroom, Zhen'ai. What is it you would like to do now?" His eyebrows raised, then lowered, as he smiled his innocent smile. He might as well have been seventeen instead of twenty-six, for the way that his facial features made him appear so much younger.

He tossed me onto the bed. I landed with a bounce and a laugh. I reached for my pillow and was tackled. "No pillow fights. How about we play house and for one night pretend that we are truly husband and wife... Would that be allowed?" His voice sounded on the verge of tears. It was only when I looked into his eyes that I saw the traces of the newly formed teardrops residing there, just shy of breaking loss from their dams.

"Yahui, my darling, I am yours. We will do tonight whatever you wish. You wish to hold me, we shall do that. If you want to tickle me silly. Tickle away. If you want to map out my features so that you can memorize them, I'm yours. I love you, husband. Let's play house."

His arm glided above my head, for a moment I waited expecting to feel his fingers combing through my hair. What actually happened was not, however, his hands in my hair, but a fluffy white pillow smacking me in the face.

Chapter 29

Who knew that *playing house* was so tiring? Obviously, not me. We were lounging in the bathing pool holding each other tightly several hours later neither one of us wanting to let the other go. I wasn't sure why he had decided to keep the play to everything but truly becoming one, but I wasn't about to complain. Although wearing a bathing suit in my own bathtub felt a little odd.

The playful games we engage in were enough to keep us both laughing and clinging tightly to each other both now and in future memories. I had never in my long existence laughed this much before.

We had swimming contests., which were so comical as the pool was only a few meters long, and the pillow fights we had prior to our time in the *pool* were something that I had only ever heard about. I never knew that it could be so fun watching the stuffing burst from the seams.

Yahui cleared his throat for the third time in the last hour.

"So how do you want to do this? I brought my laptop, so I can log onto the game. You needed me to take off the amulet. And we have long sense done that." He eyed the shining charm on the floor by the hallway door.

I sighed. Reluctantly giving my wordless acknowledgment that he was right, we couldn't keep putting this off. This was the fourth time we had talked about what would come next. Each time we got one step closer. The laptop was plugged in (Check), the amulet had been stripped of its power over him (Double Check). Now all there was to do was for me to remove my spell that was making him stay awake, and to login to the game before his body travels off to sleep.

I wasn't even sure how long it would take for one of the other lives to surface...

Sigh "I think that we need to leave the bathing pool. You are correct, we cannot put this off any longer. No matter how much I don't want this night to end. We have to remove the spell and get you into the game." I sighed again, lowering my head back onto his shoulder. "This isn't moving is it?"

"No. I don't think it is." He laughed.

"Ok let's go."

He sat still while I stood up ascending the stairs slowly and drying off. I felt his eyes watching my every move. I knew why he waited, for I felt it too. Deep in my body I yearned to feel his touch and to touch him. These things wouldn't allow us to move forward, at least not right now. So instead I donned my bathrobe, and without looking back, exited the room through the bedchamber door instead of the hallway one. That door still held recent memories that I can still picture like it was hours ago and not days.

He joined me in the bedroom a moment later. Wearing only a towel wrapped tightly around his waist. His wet boxer briefs left to dry in the bathroom.

His well-defined abs on full display, still damp with tiny droplets of water that trailed down over him. His voice sounded huskier when he spoke. Making my eyes leave his torso to meet his smoldering gaze.

"Do you think that you will give my past self what they want this evening? Could a few hours from now find our bodies entangled?"

I felt the flame of heat flood my cheeks, though I forced myself to not look away. My voice was not so strong and my words tumbled out wavering with each sound.

"Yahui, I know not. My love, please—"

"I know. I just cannot help but picture it. It is why I stopped myself all evening from. Well you know what from. I want there to be no doubt or anything hovering over us when we do finally consummate our relationship. I hope that will be after you become my real wife and not just in game.

For when we do finally join I want our union to be one that last for longer than one night before we have to go days, perhaps months, before we are able to truly love each other as we were fated to do. I vow, Zhen'ai that once this is over *we will be together*. I refuse to lose you. I will never forget you. I won't let you fade away. You are my Light in the Darkness." He toojg me into his arms. His breathy words whispered in my ear.. "Use my light to guide you from darkness if you need to. I love you."

I felt my body sway and I clung to him for support. I needed to pull myself together. If I didn't, we would never get things started tonight. I had only one hundred sixty-eight days left and those days will fly by. I needed to believe in Yahui's vow. I had to have faith that we would be together, always.

I took a deep breath, inhaling the scent of the lavender soap on his skin along with his musky normal scents. I squeezed him once more before pushing my palms onto his chest trying to distance myself away enough to look into his eyes.

"I except your vow and swear to you in return that my love for you won't fail. I will come to the virtual world as often as I can."

His crooked smile warmed me to my core. He let me go and walked to his laptop. Opening it up and entering his password, which he had changed to my name, Wu Lihwa, so that we would remember it, before Yahui walked over to the bed. Propping himself up on the headboard still wearing only the towel he waited for me expectantly.

"Um, aren't you going to get dressed?" I had just spent hours with him wearing only his underwear, yet now, now I was feeling shy? My eyes fell to the foot of the bed.

"If you want me dressed then I will get dressed, although my clothes are... well.." His head motioned to a few articles of clothing piled on the floor. I remembered now... His clothing was more than dirty and a little worse for wear as well. Shirt buttons scattered all over the bedroom floor. I giggled.

"Yeah. Ok." I smiled shyly. Conjuring clothing wasn't difficult. I just had to concentrate... I thought about the clothing that I had seen him wear before and decided on a pair of jeans and another white silk dress shirt. His eyes shimmered in the light from the laptop's screen as his once bare chest was now clothed.

His smile was so beautiful I sighed. I walked to the vanity where my own laptop sat with each step my robe transformed into my own articles of clothing. "Let's login and then I will remove my spell."

I heard Yahui laugh. "Ok. I get the feeling that you are dragging your feet my love. But if that is what you want to do..."

"Yes, I will be stripping the spell as our connection is locked. So not really dragging my feet just making sure that your soule is safe in the game before I... well you know what I'm about to do."

"I do. I know that this isn't easy for you, Zhen'ai." His fingers played along the keys and I felt the tingling of the virtual spell running through me.

"Yahui..." I watched for a second as his eyes locked with me and in them was a light that made me shiver. "Xai Yahui" I closed my eyes waiting for the tug of my magic indicating that his soule was truly locked into the game before muttering the words that would break the spell. "Dispel insomnia... Sleep."

§

"I thought you weren't coming." His playful sing-song voice washed over the underlying sounds of the stream near a small stone cottage.

"Sorry to keep you waiting," I smiled "husband."

"Come here my wife. Let me hold you for a moment longer, then my heart you must leave me."

I shook my head frantically. "No," I said.

"My love, my beautiful Goddess Zhen'ai. You must," he said. Finally, he brought his arms up reaching for me. Once his hands found their quarry he pulled me into his strong embrace. Sliding his gentle hand through my hair attempting to tame the strands that were whirling around my tear soaked face. "Tears, real tears? Oh Zhen'ai. Stop crying.You need to figure out who in fact has surfaced."

I choked back a sob I hadn't realized was forming. I knew that this was coming, yet I feared this moment more than I had known. Once I left here I would be the only person in the house who knew what was about to transpire. I still had failed to tell Ayi.

I was sure that she would try to be a voice of reason... A voice that would attempt to talk me out of doing this.. Wrapped in his arms I wept. I wept for the days that we had been robbed of. I wept for the injustice of a god who was spiteful and cruel. But most of all I wept because I knew that once I left him here and returned to the real world I would be faced with one of the past lives that I had loved. Still loved...Reopening old wounds in an attempt to save this perfect fated love. This love that had me pressed tightly in his arms...

"Shhhh my heart. Please stop crying... I will be alright. I know that you will be back for me."

"I will, I promise..." I wiped my cheeks with my hands. "Yahui, I am so sor—"

"Don't you dare apologize. You have nothing to be sorry for." He laughed, it started out as a light hearted chuckle but soon it developed into a full belly laugh. It turned out to be contagious, and I didn't even know why we were laughing, but soon, we both clung to each other and to our aching sides.

"You up for making a wager?" he said after his laughter had fully subsided.

"A wager? What are we betting on?" My interest peaked.

"Let's wager on who will come forward first." His eyes stared at me. The laughter that had been there a minute ago was gone, Now he was all business.

"Okay. Who do you think will come through first?"

"No," He shook his head a slight chuckle passing over his perfect lips. "That isn't how our wager works. Let us go over the stakes. If I win you will need to come here to me for a full twenty-four hours in game time. That will be, what, less than three minutes in the real world."

"Okay, and if I win?" I smiled thinking of what I wanted to give him. For no matter what I would still do these things and more. "If I win we shall build a new in game residence and you will teach me how to level up all my skills. That should take a while to accomplish."

He smiled my most favorite smile. "Sounds like whichever way that this wager goes I win."

I nodded. "Plus I modified the spell. You won't be here for years, my love. The slowing of time, irl, is for only when I am here with you." Although I even took it one step further. By making his time in game alone actually pass by slower than the time I would be living through. For him when I leave here it will be mere hours before he sees me again. Yet for me. It could actually be days.

The relief that shined on his face was evident.

"That is wonderful to hear. I thought I would be an old man by the time we were able to get through the first week." He leaned onto the stone wall of the cottage. "I think it will be Yang. "

"Yang? Why do you think that?" I wasn't sure I was ready to encounter *him*.

"Because once he understood what was at stake he was the most vocal. Is vocal even the right term?" Yahui took my hand into his pulling me to him. "Now who do you think it will be?"

"I think it will be Mai Jung. I think that the ones who had love in their lives will want to return to them. If Jung is one of the many who are in your head, then he will bow out first."

"Interesting. I'm not sure how many of the Twenty are in my body, but I understand your theory." His smile warmed my weary soule. He placed his arms on my shoulders giving me his adorable mischievous grin. "Now we seal our wager."

"How do we do that? What happens if we are both wrong?"

"Well, I think we should kiss to seal it, and if we are both wrong," he pressed his lips to mine. We kissed fiercely, and by the time we parted, I had forgotten what we had been talking about. But Yahui hadn't.

"If we are both wrong," he said, "lets both pray that it isn't Wu Xia."

One hundred and sixty-seven days remain.

Epilogue

Silence.

Deafening silence.

That is what my master used to call it. When all other sounds were stripped away and all that you had left were the other senses.

I was unable to see anything either. It was so dark, too dark. I tried to recall the last memory that I had. I was holding someone and I declared my love.

Who was that someone?

I could almost picture the lips. The way that the hair fell to the side. The curve of the jaw. Such perfection. I felt my lungs fill with a large intake of air, yet I didn't recognize the scents. It was floral, perhaps. Why can't I hear anything? Why can't I see?

My lungs filled again, and I felt in my chest a welcome sensation. *Right now I need to feel anything, something.* Again I concentrated on my love. The way the skin felt. Yes, it was as soft as silk. That is what it was. Silk.

I felt that now, too. Thank the gods! My hand moved, another small blessing, over the smooth soft surface of silk. *Was I wearing it?* I willed my eyes to open, yet I neither felt them move nor did I see anything.

I, in turn, decided to concentrate, once again, on my love. The amazing smile, the way it lights up even the blackest of nights. *That is what I need.* I needed that smile. I could see the way lips moved when they spoke and the small little dimple that formed when they laughed. That laugh sounded like the bells in the temple.

I hear something. A low chiming, it was so faint, at first I thought it was my mind playing tricks. I heard it again, and it was louder. Clearer. My heart raced. Whatever afflicted me was wearing off. Perhaps it's me remembering my love.

I turned all of my concentration into recalling more about my love.

Yes, I see them now—those eyes, the color of cherry blossoms.

She is beautiful! I can't recall her name.

What is her name?

Master, help me to remember!

I hear a soft voice carried on a slight breeze.

"What is your name?"

Mine? No that isn't what I want to know. I must recall her name.

My name has no consequence.

"Who are you?" says the whisper again...

I am a man, a warrior for my Lord! My name? Her name?

Everything is fuzzy. Why can't I remember?

She has beautiful eyes. The color of cherry blossoms. I remember that.

My eyes! A flash of color. Red? Another flash.

"Awaken," the soft hauntingly familiar voice rings in my ears. "Tell me your name?" So sweet a sound.

I take a deep breath, opening my lips. Praying that I will be able to answer her sweet request. "My name—"

A battle ground, smoke billowing from the fires of a burning hut.

A temple with my love's beautiful face. My Goddess.

"My name is Wu. Wu Xia"

All is silent, except for the sound of my heart in my ears. Once more, I will my eyes to open. This time they obey. My love. my Goddess. My Zhen'ai.

She is here, in this place.

Instinctively, I sweep the surroundings. We are in a bedchamber. This must be the room of my goddess, for I have never seen such luxury before. Fine silk fabric forms a canopy above our heads. The frame of the bed is a dark wood I am unfamiliar with.

When my eyes land on Zhen'ai, she is dressed in such unusual attire. A memory pulls at my thoughts, but I can't quite recall it.

"Welcome back my love. We need to talk. What do you remember?" Zhen'ai's face looked troubled. Her eyes were puffy, had she been crying? Who made my love cry? They will rue the day that they crossed me!

Carefully I consider her word. Memories like a flash of

lightning in the sky flash briefly at first.

"I remember you," I see Zhen'ai standing pressed against my body. Sharing a lovers kiss. "I remember *us*."

Then another not so pleasant memory of bodies littering the forest floor. "My men?"

It all came flooding back. Her beautiful face trying to explain...

"I died. Why am I back?"

Zhen'ai sat with her legs pulled to her chest. Her legs were covered by such an odd material. Her eyes darted from her hands to my face, several times before she replied.

"Xia, it was Longwei he brought you back into the body of your most recent reincarnation.He brought back several of you in fact. As punishment to me. It's always been my punishment... For I've loved you through so many reincarnations."

"Longwei." The name made more memories wash over me and not all were mine. Yet, I saw them with these eyes. The eyes of my soule's host. The eyes of Zhen'ai's love.

I clenched my hands into tight fists, while my heart raced pounding my blood, thumping a rhythm in my ears. I felt a heat wash over me. Looking up, I saw the fear in Zhen'ai's eyes. *I mustn't scare her.* I try to calm myself, but I am failing miserably. When I finally spoke, my words were rough and harsh, much too harsh, and through clenched teeth.

"Yes," the word rumbled out of my throat over my lips.

"I remember."

Acknowledgements

Firstly I want to take this time to give my heartfelt appreciation to a group of people to whom I owe sooo much. And without whom this book would have never been made. I will list out these incredible people here and I am extremely sorry if I don't get all of your names. That is the beauty of having a series. I have many opportunities to include everyone.

William (Bill) Lindie Jr. , Betty Jane (Soule) Lindie, John Daniel Harriman Jr, Kevin William Harriman, Debora Marie (Lindie) Weigelt and her husband Alden and their beautiful family (Shawn, Megan and Erica) which is ever growing. I can't forget Miss Thyme!), Karen Elizabeth (Lindie) Kinder, her husband Joe, and Nicole (Kinder) Curry not to mention all of the fur babies and little Einstein, Michael Allen Lindie His beautiful Wife Lou Ann (DiBlasi) Lindie and Jessie, James and Lucky (Who is greatly missed)...William Allen Lindie III and his wife Chris (Armstrong) Lindie and Brandon Way, David Allen Lindie his wife Jody (Shank) Lindie and their two boys (Ryan and Justin) and their ever growing fetching Lindie Family. Sharon Jane (Lindie) Stalker and her family, Dan, Matthew, and Katie, Debra (Ames) Farris and family, Polly Anna Watson, Elizabeth Doll, Robert T. Canipe and Redhawk Publishing, Robert Womack, Dan Smith, Rae Jenkins, Amber D. Watts, Jeff Kiefer, Becca Calloway and everyone with the Hickory NANO and Writers group... The Foothill Writers Group. Diane Little. And the list goes on and on. I could sit here for the next two months and write down names every day and still not be done. I have been truly Blessed!

My amazing parents, William (Bill) Lindie Jr. and Betty Jane (Soule) Lindie, who not only brought me into this world but gifted me with the love of books and words. I love you! Without you both, this book would have never been written, in more ways than one.

Thank You, Mom for encouraging me to take that leap back into the world of school books and long nights of studying to chase after my dream with no fear. Little did we know that it would turn out this way. I know you can see me as I make ready to fully realize my dream I shared with you all those years ago. I love and miss you sovery much.

Thank you, Daddy... for loving me, supporting me and encouraging me and for listening to me go on and on about my book. And for believing in me enough that you trusted me to work on yours, I love you...

Growing up the youngest of seven children in Winslow, Maine (until I was in seventh grade when I moved with my parents to a small rural town called Thorndike). Words have long been my faithful companion. By the time of the move I was no stranger to rhyme and tempo. Having written many poems and song lyrics. Though it was here, at Mount View Jr High, that I penned my very first short story: *The Moose is Loose in Bangor Maine;* for my seventh grade English teacher (Please forgive my forgetful mind as I cannot recall your name, but I want to take the time to thank you none-the-less)... and with that 'A' the writing *bug* was jump-started into full swing.

Everyone at some point in their lives experiences loss. I am no stranger to the hardships of grief. Having lost both of my Grandmothers early in my life. These losses were followed by multiple Aunts and Uncles as the years passed as well. Of course not to be forgotten the only Grandfather that I had ever known

Ellery Soule (Seeing that my grandpa Lindie (William Allen Lindie Sr.) died when my dad was just a wee lad). Yet it is the unexpected losses that can have the most profound effects on you.

In the summer of 2015 my family lost our rock, our cornerstone, our key stone if you will... and it shook the foundation of our family to its very core.

My mother was diagnosed with cancer and was taken by it within a few days of the diagnosis. My Dad and siblings all shared in that devastating blow, only to have cancer claim my beautiful and talented sister Karen in 2016. As you have already seen, in the very front of this book, I have dedicated this first book in my *Fated Soules* series to those two incredible ladies!

I want to thank my two sons, John and Kevin, who have been so very patient with me as I have worked on not only writing this book but also doing up the illustrations. Sometimes well into the wee hours of the morning. Thank you for supporting me and I love you both very much.

Also thank you Kevin and John for bringing the world of Anime into my life. Without which I never would have started drawing. While I am talking about Anime I must also thank Antonio Ippolito. Who broadened my 'scope', and who took the time to help me catalogue anime characters.

Thank you to John Sr. for being there when I needed you, and even though we are no longer together. Thank you for being a friend through it all.

Thank you to all my sisters and brothers... Gosh we are a crew. You all have loved me and shown your support and admiration. There are truly no words to adequately express my thanks. Thank you Deb, Kay, Mike, Billy, David, and Sharon (a special thank you to Sharon for taking the time to help me with this endeavor by reading the early draft of my book), you all are more than just my siblings you are my life coaches and cheerleaders. I love you all and miss you more than you all know. I don't want my extended family (cousins and such) to think that I have forgotten about you... I have not. Nor would I ever. You are all so very important in my life.

Thank you to the amazing teachers I have had along the way...Not only in my sixth through twelfth grade years, but also the incredible instructors who have gifted my life. From the lovely ladies at the Hair Academy (Jody Arno an incredible woman who not only can cut hair, but has shown what courage is. And she is a strong influence in the lengths one will go for love) ...

To the extremely supportive instructors at CVCC: Polly Anna Watson who now is employed at CPCC, you have been a burst of welcome Joy I can never thank you enough for all that you have done in the creation of this book. From Listening to me read you every word. To assisting me with my editing. Also thanking for being a very dear friend!

The Write Stuff Creative writing group... Oh the memories of getting this group (club) off the ground. I am so proud of how far they have come.

Thank you to all the members of the creative writing classes with Robert Womack, Andrew, Kylie, Jonathan, Patrick, Sierra, Ladasha, for making me feel that I could actually, maybe, possibly write....I know I am forgetting some, I humbly ask you to please forgive me. Ariel Hamilton, for giving me the courage to stand infront of a crowd and give a presentation.

Thank you Elizabeth Doll for taking the time to not only befriend me, but to mentor me with art. With your help I grew in ways I never dreamed possible. You have played such a pivotal role. Reading my story, and critiquing my art. Thank you.

Thank you to Dan Smith for teaching me so very much

about art and being unafraid to try new media, also for allowing me to just do my 'Arting'. I will be forever grateful. Amber D. Watts... You are an incredible artist. Thank you for making me think outside the box as well. Jeff Kiefer, who believed in me enough to allow me to make up the time lost from illnesses, as well as the returns of the tumors that brought me to Art in the first place.

Oddly enough here is a very special thank you to the high school English teacher who told me I would never be a writer.

Look at me now!

Thank you Debra (Ames) Farris. We have been through so very much together over the last twenty-four years. Thank you for listening to my stories. And for always being there when I needed a mental health check. I love and miss you.

Thank you, Sonja (Butler) Richardson... Gosh you have been my friend forever it seems. We didn't get the name of terror twins for nothing. And even though we haven't talked much the last few months you still played a pivotal role in giving me the courage to write. Thank you Terror Twin!

I want to thank Robert Canipe and everyone at Redhawk Publishing. For not only believing in me enough to publish this book, but also in helping me every step of the way through this publishing process. To Rae Jenkins who, sweetie you are amazing. The hardest part of writing a book is not the words. For the words flow like the river to the ocean. It's the editing! Thank you so very much.

I would also Like to thank God for the many blessings that he has brought into my life. The art work in this book from the cover art to the chapter headers the ability to do them all came from Him... I am forever humbled by this gift.

It may seem that this has gone on and on, and as I sit here

I know that I could continue. I want to let you know that If you have played a role in this process at all you are greatly appreciated.

Lastly, I want to thank you, my readers. You are the greatest! Thank you for picking this book up and reading it. I will have the next installment of the *Fated Soules* series out as soon as I can and still give you all a great story.

Respectfully Yours,

Jan Lindie

About the Author

JAN LINDIE is a native Mainer who transplanted to North Carolina in 2010 with her two sons. Jan loves to spend time with her sons, family, and friends, as well as traveling home to Maine as often as she can.

Jan enjoys researching her family's Genealogy as much as she loves to write and work on her illustrations.

Jan graduated from Catawba Valley Community College's Associate of Art's program where she studied Creative Writing before transferring over to the Associates of Fine Arts: Visual Art degree.

As a professional Artist, Jan has had her art displayed in the Art Counsel and at Taste Full Beans Coffeehouse in downtown Hickory, NC.

Jan's art is also beautifully displayed in the book and Bible study *Joy Actions* written by PollyAnna Joy, as well as in a book of poetry *View from Tuff-end* written by Bill Lindie. She also had art published in CVCC's Literary Journal *Sanctuary* for three consecutive years. Both *Joy Actions* and *Sanctuary* can be purchased through Amazon.com.

Jan's own debut novel *From Darkness*, the first book in her *Fated Soules* series, combines her artistry in both words and images. *From Darkness* can also be purchased from Amazon, Barnes and Noble.com, The CVCC Campus Store (bookstore. cvcc.edu) and through local events.

Check for updated information on Jan's Facebook page at https://www.facebook.com/jan.lindieauthor

Made in the USA
Monee, IL
24 August 2020